John Bunyan's
A PILGRIM'S PROGRESS

FOREWORD

John Bunyan was born in 1628, just a few years after the death of Shakespeare. He became a tinker, like his father, but when the Civil War broke out, was drafted into Cromwell's army of Roundheads (the Parliamentarians). In 1649, home from the war, he married a girl as poor as himself, whose dowry consisted of just two books: *The Plain Man's Pathway to Heaven* and *Practice of Piety*. Reading these wrought such an upheaval in John's soul that his life was transformed. He joined a Christian fellowship and began to preach. Lay preaching (by people other than clergymen) was illegal at that time, and Bunyan was arrested and sent to Bedford prison for 12 years.

He spent those years writing – six books in all – before the Declaration of Indulgence in 1672 brought him his freedom. Religious tolerance was short-lived. Though Bunyan had time to become a licensed preacher, the Declaration was cancelled within the year and John was re-arrested.

This time his gaol sentence was only six months, and he put them to good use. In his prison cell he wrote a first draft of *The Pilgrim's Progress*. A later, second volume told the story of Christiana and her children – the progress of a woman pilgrim.

The last 16 years of his life were happy. He became pastor of Bedford, and saw his books being widely read. One night, after a 70-mile ride through torrential rain, he was taken ill and died. His grave is in Bunhill Fields, last resting place of the bravest and best of English non-Conformists.

For St Gabriel and all his angels
G.M.

To Maria
J.C.

First published in the United States in 2005 by
The Overlook Press, Peter Mayer Publishers, Inc.
Woodstock & New York

WOODSTOCK:
One Overlook Drive
Woodstock, NY 12498
www.overlookpress.com
[for individual orders, bulk and special sales, contact our Woodstock office]

NEW YORK:
141 Wooster Street
New York, NY 10012

Text copyright © Geraldine McCaughrean 1999
Illustrations copyright © Jason Cockroft 1999

Cataloging-in-Publication Data is available from the Library of Congress

Printed in China

ISBN 1-58567-638-1

1 3 5 7 9 8 6 4 2

John Bunyan's
A PILGRIM'S PROGRESS

Retold by Geraldine McCaughrean
Illustrated by Jason Cockcroft

One

THE
GREAT ESCAPE

*In which I dream
of Christian,
and Christian dreams
of escape*

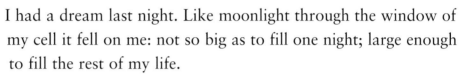

I had a dream last night. Like moonlight through the window of my cell it fell on me: not so big as to fill one night; large enough to fill the rest of my life.

I dreamed that I saw myself – no, someone very like me – a man. He was standing at his garden gate, bent under the weight of a great knapsack, and in his hand was a guidebook. Had someone passing the gate thrust the book into his hand? I don't know: dreams never start at the beginning. Plainly he had never opened the book till now.

As he read, all the colour drained from his face; a ghastly, clammy terror made him sweat. I know it: I felt it in my own palms. He wept, too, and shook, like a rainy willow tree. The breath sobbed in his throat, louder and louder, till he clapped the book shut and hugged it to his chest, rocking to and fro in agonies of fright. Then, turning his face up towards the sky, he howled,

'WHAT AM I GOING TO DO?'

He struggled to take off the knapsack, but it seemed so tightly strapped to his shoulders that he could not be free of it. And yet I sensed that it was new to him; he had only been wearing it for as long as he had been holding the book in his hands.

In his agitation, he rushed indoors, seized hold of his mother, who was stringing beans, and spun her round. 'We must get out of here!' he panted. 'We must! We must!'

'Christian! What is it, dear? What's the matter? Why are you wearing that bag?'

But when he saw her tired, anxious face, and how his father looked up startled from eating, Christian could not bear to strike the same fear into them as he himself felt. He had to keep the terrible news to himself – a secret pent up inside him. It burned in there like a fever. It grew inside him like a pain, until his face ran with sweat and he struck out at the furniture with his fists.

'Is that any way to carry on?' said his mother, struggling in vain to pull the knapsack off his shoulders. 'Whatever's the matter with you? Calm down!'

Christian went to bed that night, but the ceiling over him seemed scrawled with nightmares, his brain scalded by dreadful thoughts. He tossed and moaned and rent the bedclothes, so that his neighbours, beyond the wall, thought he must be dying.

'No wonder you can't sleep, boy,' grumbled his father, poking his head round the door. 'Look at you – wearing that great silly pack in bed! Take it off, can't you? Anyone would think you were making ready for a journey, not a night's sleep!' His mother came to the doorway, too, bleary-faced, woken by the noise.

So at last Christian decided he must share it with them, share the appalling contents of that book. He had them sit down on the end of the bed, and explained as gently as possible, 'We have to leave here. We have to get out. This city – this whole everywhere – our home – everybody living hereabouts – it's all going to be destroyed. A terrible destruction is coming – I don't know when exactly, but soon. We have to go somewhere – I'm not sure where, yet, or how to get there, but we just have to . . .'

His father herrumphed and scowled, 'Is this a joke?'

'Hush, Christian dear,' said his mother soothingly, patting his hand. 'You're not well. You get some sleep. You'll feel better in the morning.'

And they treated him as if he were ill, as if fever was making him hallucinate. They confined him to bed, where he lay weeping and groaning with helpless frustration. The neighbours came to peer in at the windows, concerned, or simply nosy.

When he did not get any better, his friends and relations tried to make him see sense by shouting at him, laughing at him, ignoring him; and Christian withdrew into himself, more lonely and terrified than a man marooned on a raft at sea.

In the end, he found it better to roam around the fields, with only the rain for company and the contemptuous hiss of wet grass. At least there he could cry out loud from time to time, '*What must I do to be saved?*'

Several times, he set off to run but, not knowing which way to run, his steps petered to a halt.

Then, one day, a stranger came up to him in the fields – a clerical man to judge by the white tabs of his cravat – and asked what the matter was.

Christian tried to steady himself, so as not to appear lunatic. 'I have read, sir, in this book, that I am condemned to die.'

The stranger shrugged, as if this were an everyday occurrence, utterly unremarkable. 'Well? What's so terrible about that?' was his response. 'An end to life's hardships, surely?'

Christian brandished the book under his nose. '*But it says here I shall have to account for my life – the kind of man I am – the state of my soul! I'm not ready! I'm not fit!*'

'In that case,' said Preacher, 'I'd run if I were you.' And he gave Christian a parchment scroll which, when opened, simply read: RUN FOR YOUR LIFE!

'Run where?' said Christian weakly.

'To the City of Gold, naturally. Haven't you read about it in the guidebook?'

'I never got past the first chapter,' Christian admitted sheepishly. 'The part about the destruction of this city here. And me.'

'Oh, read on, sir! Do! Read on, at your leisure,' said Preacher, his stern face betraying at last a certain amused twinkle behind his eyes. 'Pilgrims are setting off every day for the City of Gold. Who wouldn't want to go there? Perpetual bliss? Sublime happiness? Everlasting life? I'm bound there myself, in good time, but, of course, I have work to do first. You, on the other hand, haven't a moment to lose. I can't guarantee you will survive the journey: it's no afternoon stroll. But then you

won't be any worse off, will you? And even if *you* fail, the City of Gold will not. Its walls will never crumble, and its delights are enough to satisfy the hungriest traveller . . . Don't lose that scroll, mind. Without it, you will not be allowed in . . . What? Are you still here?'

'B-but . . . which way must I . . . ?' stammered Christian.

Preacher pointed across the fields. 'You see that little white wicket gate?'

Christian tried to see. He tried so hard that his feet lifted clear off the ground. 'No. No! I don't see a thing!'

'Well, then, do you see that light shining?'

'I . . . er . . . I think so.'

'Go straight towards it. By and by, you'll reach the gate. Knock. Someone will point you the way to go.' As he spoke, Preacher tucked his fingers into the front of Christian's dishevelled coat; Christian thought he must be helping himself to the price of a meal from Christian's wallet, but in fact he was pushing something into it instead. 'A key. You may need it.' Then he turned away.

Christian began to run – haltingly at first, glancing back over his shoulder, and then fixing his eye on the glimmer – like the sunlight on a cottage window – and running towards it, his rucksack banging up and down, the parchment scroll gripped in his fist like a runner's baton. Past the outlying houses of the city he ran, catching the eye of various neighbours out in their gardens. Some called out, some grinned and twirled their fingers beside their foreheads: 'Look, there goes crack-brained Christian!'

Two actually took to their heels and ran alongside him, asking where he was off to, who was chasing him. He found Ob Stinate puffing along on his right, Mr Bendy on his left, both plying him with questions.

Christian panted out his dreadful news.
'Destruction! . . . The end! . . . Condemned!'
And now that he knew where to head, he felt
honour-bound to urge them. 'Come with me!'

'What, and leave our homes and families and
everything dear to us?' snorted Ob Stinate.

'Yes! What good are any of those things
to a dead man?'

'Well, have you got anything better
to offer?' asked Ob.

'Yes! Safety! Happiness! Endless!
Wonders!' He could not keep up this
pace. He would have to slow down.

'Sounds good to me,' said
Mr Bendy. 'Tell me more.'

So Christian told him – showed
him the guidebook and the scroll,
wildly excited now about the good
things in store, rather than dwelling
on the fear he had left behind.
His excitement was infectious;
Mr Bendy's eyes began to shine with the
same eagerness. But Ob Stinate was not so
quick to change the thinking of a lifetime.

'He doesn't know what he's talking
about! I mean to say – has he ever been
to this "Golden City"? What does he
know, blast him! How far is he going
to get with that pack on his back? He's
pipe-dreaming. It's a nonsense. Give up
everything I know and love for some
hare-brained scheme? No fear! You take
my word, Bendy: Christian is leading
you astray. Don't you listen to him!'

15

And, like a man with his belt caught round the bedpost, Ob Stinate slowed suddenly and stopped, retracing his footsteps towards the city of Destruction.

But Mr Bendy was content to go on jogging alongside Christian. After days of being shunned and lonely, having company lifted Christian's spirits enormously. And if he squinnied up his eyes and peered, he could almost persuade himself he saw the little white wicket gate . . .

The land ahead was green – as emerald green as the back of a toad, against the darker fields and forests. The soil under their feet was springy and damp – spongy – quaggy even. But Christian and Bendy were running at such a pace that, by the time they realised the truth, they had already gone too far out. They were already knee-deep and staggering, pitching and plunging, the bog's mud sucking at their boots, the ooze slopping in over their boot-tops, sucking hungrily at their thighs, dragging them in deeper and down . . .

Two

THE
GREAT BOG MISERY

*In which Christian
gets bogged down
and led astray*

'Is this one of your "marvellous wonders"?' spluttered Bendy, his face flecked with mud as he thrashed about in the mire. 'Is this your idea of happiness?'

Christian could not answer him; the weight of the pack on his back, and the lack of a firm foothold, meant he was pitched over backwards to flounder like a turtle on its shell, while the mire sucked at his hair and crawled in at his ears. The very mud seemed to be infested – alive with whispering and whimpering – a soughing slough of sorrow, a morass of misery. As it gripped Christian's ribs, his heart gripped with horror and the sure knowledge that he was doomed. All his brave hopes of reaching the Golden City were leeching out of him into the Bog. 'Help me, Bendy! For God's sake, help me!' he pleaded, since his neighbour, having no pack, was at least vertical – sinking, but on his feet.

'Help you? Damned if I will!' said Bendy, wading back the way he had come. 'You got me into this. It's all your fault. Why didn't I listen to Ob Stinate?'

'Help! Bendy! Don't leave me!'

'To think I quit home and family for this! Never been so miserable in my entire life!'

Neither had Christian. Even back in Destruction City, he had not suffered this kind of desolate disappointment. To have come such a short way and to meet with such complete defeat! It was enough to make a man weep. When he screwed his head round, Bendy was nowhere to be seen, and Christian was still within sight of home.

He reached the edge, but could not scramble out. Time and again, the quagmire dragged him back in. Its whispering rose to a roaring in his ears. He lifted his chin, opened his mouth to cry out, but the slurry spilled in over his lower lip . . .

'Here. Give me your hand.'

Christian's eyes just then were blinded with tears. The stranger seemed immeasurably tall, towering over a reptilian, squirming Christian, but it was simply that he was standing on firm ground. Christian reached out to grasp his hand, but with fingers so slippery and a misery so crippling that he sobbed, 'I can't do it! Leave me! I'm a lost man!'

'Why didn't you use the steps?' said the stranger, calmly hauling Christian out by the collar of his coat.

'I was running so fast. I never . . . What steps?'

'There are patches of safe ground – like stepping stones – right across the Bog. Don't you have the guidebook? There's a map in there. Difficult to read for a beginner, I know. Apparently lots of people come to grief here. Allow me to introduce myself. My name is Faithful – a handyman by profession.'

As he crouched on hands and knees, and fear drained out of his clothes, along with the mud, Christian was left feeling angry and abused. 'What's it doing here? I mean to say, why don't the Authorities fill it in – a great bog like this, right across the Pilgrim's Way. It's a disgrace!'

'Oh, they do, they do,' said Faithful. 'The King sends cartloads of hardcore down here every day, for tipping into the swamps. Advice, wisdom, experience, old heads, visions, books, saints, art, parables . . . Twenty thousand cartloads, to my certain knowledge. But the Bog is growing at the same time, and it just swallows it all up. Such a shame.'

As Christian recovered, he saw the truth of this. Every few minutes, a cart came rattling down to the far side of the Bog laden with stone statues of saints, plaster madonnas, oil paintings in heavy gilt frames, whole libraries of books bound in red morocco, the rubble of ruined buildings, and any amount of beautiful quarried marble. It was all dumped into the Great Bog to try and turn it to solid

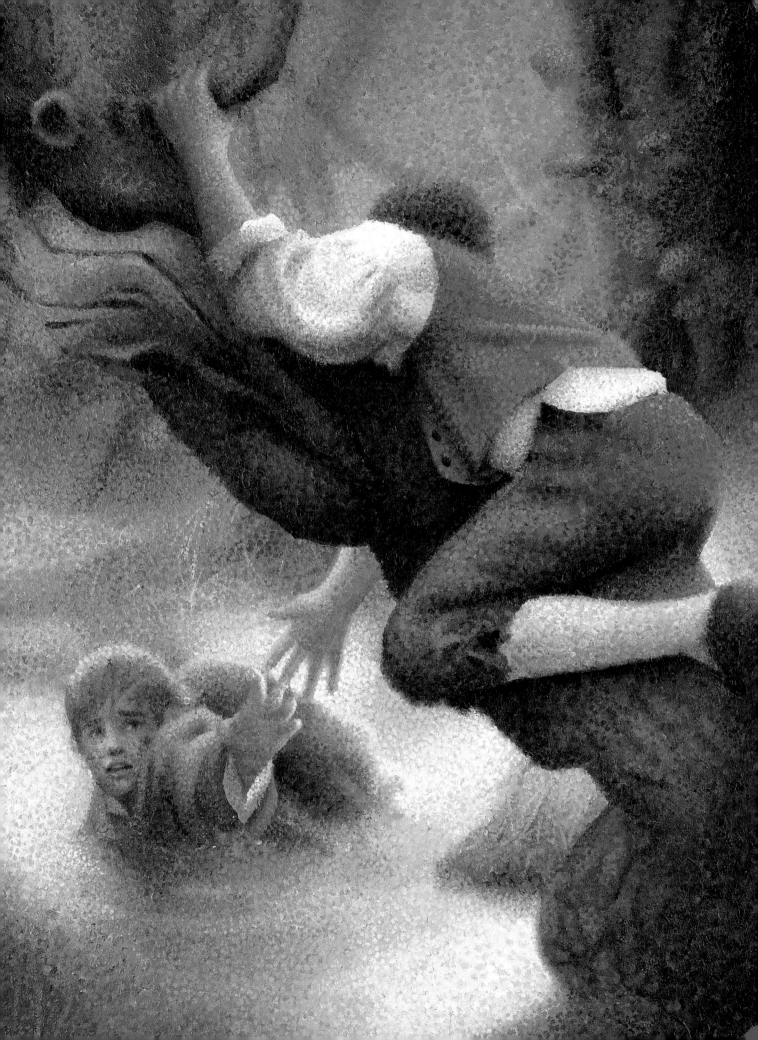

ground. But running into it off the fields was so much putrid slurry that the green bog continued to bubble like a stewpot, and never grew any smaller.

'Apparently, all the doubts and fears and misgivings and worries of the world trickle down into this sinkhole,' Faithful explained. 'There's nothing the King can do about it. It's a natural phenomenon. Lucky I came by just now. I'm a new pilgrim myself, but I read about this place in the guidebook last night. I'll leave you to rest and get cleaned up. Perhaps we'll meet up again, further along the Way?' And off he went, whistling cheerfully, before Christian could properly thank him for saving him from the Great Bog Misery.

Alec Smart knew where the stepping stones were. Christian was just puzzling over the map in the book, when up came Alec Smart, a dapper, well-dressed man who gave the impression he had travelled to and from the Golden City dozens of times without the smallest mishap. Christian imagined he must have arrived there on one of the King's carts, for he had such a royal air of authority about him.

'Seem to have got yourself into a pretty pickle,' said the jovial Mr Smart.

'I fell in the Bog,' said Christian (which was blatantly obvious as the mud on top of his head set to a piecrust).

'Want to know a short cut?'

'Ooh, I don't er . . . Preacher told me I should . . .'

'Oh, him,' said Alec. 'He'd like to think he's the only one who knows the way to the City of Gold. No, no. If you go up yonder, it'll take days off your journey. Weeks. And you'll avoid the wicket gate: save all that knocking. Of course, the first thing you ought to do . . . that's if you don't mind a word of advice from a man of the world?'

'Oh, not at all! Most grateful,' said Christian hastily.

'First thing you want to do is get rid of that pack. Such a drag on a travelling man. Slow you down. Big nuisance.'

Christian explained his difficulty – how the rucksack had come with the book, how he could not get it unfastened.

'And what's in it, if I may be so bold as to ask?'

Christian blushed. He hated to think of the filthy refuse and offal, the dirty washing and blotted copybooks he knew were crammed into his rucksack. 'Oh, just my Past,' he mumbled, shamefaced. 'My sins.'

'I know just the man for you, then! Along that path I told you, there's a house. People there. Sister and brother of mine. Name of Dodge and Quibble. They'll soon show you how to get it off. Got an answer to every problem, those two. Say Alec sent you.'

So Christian thanked Alec Smart and hurried off along the path, to be rid of his pack and reach the Golden City all the quicker.

The path petered out.

At first Christian thought he had made a mistake – that he was not perhaps as clever as Mr Smart, and had strayed off the path. He got out the guidebook. But it did not even show the path.

Soon he found himself in a forest – could barely see the wood for the trees – and when he emerged on the other side, he was confronted by a hillside criss-crossed with a maze of identical pathways. Sheep bleated gormlessly at him, and blinked their yellow eyes.

The further Christian went, the steeper the hill's ragged top loomed, until, like a breaking tidal wave, it reared up and over him, blocking out the sky entirely. He had reached a dead end.

'The whole mountain is going to fall on me!' thought Christian. 'What an utter fool I was not to follow the straight path! At least then I had that light to guide me. I must have been mad to believe that know-all know-nothing, Smart.' And he would have beaten his head against the beetling cliff in self-disgust, if he had not been so scared of bringing an avalanche down on top of him. Skidding down the slope on the tails of his coat, his heavy pack banging round his ears, Christian fled.

'Why didn't you do as you were told? Now you'll have to start all over again.' The voice was wonderfully familiar. Christian looked up and saw Preacher sitting in a tree on the edge of the wood, his face dark with disapproval.

'Oh, I'm so sorry. I'm really, really sorry! It's just that I met this gentleman, Mr Smart . . .'

'Ah! Alec Smart,' said Preacher nodding, continuing to frown.

'Bendy deserted me, and I couldn't make Ob Stinate see sense, and I stink to high heaven 'cause I fell in the Bog, and now – and now . . .' His voice tailed off, and he dropped his hands disconsolately, and hung his head. 'I'm just no good at this. No good at all.'

Preacher jumped down out of the tree and put an arm round Christian. 'Never say die, lad. There's no mistake you've made today that hasn't been made by others before you. The great thing is not to give up, not to fall by the wayside. Back to the straight-and-narrow way, now, and keep right along it as far as the wicket gate. Be brave. I won't say it gets easier further on, but you have learned some useful lessons, and the Gate Keeper can teach you a thing or two more.'

So grateful was Christian for a second chance, and so humbled by his foolish mistake, that he thought he could face any trial, any hardship, any privation, in order to reach the City of Gold.

The daylight failed round him. The distant light glimmered beckoningly. And Christian, as he got over his fright, and was troubled by the blisters on his feet, stopped pondering glory and gave his mind to practical matters. 'I hope that Gate Keeper offers me a bite of supper. I'm absolutely famished.'

Three

THE
MUSEUM OF WONDERS

*In which Christian
knocks, and is shown
some marvellous
sights*

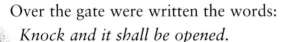

Over the gate were written the words:
Knock and it shall be opened.

Christian knocked, and the gate was opened. Simple as that.
He could hardly believe anything was so easy. He glimpsed
a face, and then a hand shot round the door and grabbed
his wrist, pulling him indoors.

At the selfsame moment, there was a thud, and an arrow
struck the gate just where his knuckles had knocked.

'What was that?' squeaked Christian, his hand to his throat.

'Oh. Forgive the suddenness of your welcome, pilgrim,'
said the Gate Keeper. 'It's just that the Enemy has a tower quite
close by. His archers try to pick off pilgrims as they stand at the
door, so I don't tend to stand on ceremony. Are you on your
own? Ah well. Sometimes dozens, sometimes one. Welcome to the
Pilgrim's Way. You'll find hospitality at the Museum of Wonders.
Just up there on the right.'

'Any chance you might help me off with my . . . ?' But the Gate
Keeper had gone, as cheerful and welcoming as the sunshine but (like the sunshine)
finished for the day.

So Christian presented himself at the Museum, a large building with no
curtains, so that the light inside streamed out on to the street. 'I'm afraid I have
no money on me to pay for bed and board,' he began apologetically.

'No matter,' said the Curator. 'You can earn your supper, if you are handy with a broom.'

As he stepped inside, Christian could not help noticing a magnificent painting which hung on the hall wall opposite the door – the portrait of a man holding a book and a scroll, looking upwards into a beam of light. The face was saintly, a slight smile playing on its lips. It was also faintly familiar to Christian, who felt he had seen a face very like it quite recently – if he could only remember where. 'Tomorrow may I see some of the exhibits in your museum?' he enquired.

But instead of an answer, a broom was thrust at him, and he was shown into a small dark room where, by sweeping up, he understood he could earn his night's lodging.

Sweeping up? He practically needed a shovel! Dust lay as thick as snow on every stick of furniture. The carpet was grey with it, and tussocks of dust sprouted up from under his feet. Once he had begun sneezing, he could not stop. The fire-grate had overspilled in grey saltpans of ash, and the mantelpiece was peopled by the clogged and blurred shapes of ornaments buried in years of dust.

The moment Christian flicked his broom about, the dust flew up in choking clouds. He tried to pat it down, fan it aside, but it eddied round him in smoky swathes, making him cough and water at the eyes. He looked about him in panic, took his cap off and tried to subdue the clouds of fluff and grit, but the more he flapped, the more dirt he disturbed and the darker the room grew in the swirling duststorm.

Suddenly a door opened, and a young woman came in, holding a bowl of water. Without a word to Christian, she began dipping in her fingertips and sprinkling waterdrops around. Then she took the broom out of his hand. Dampened, the dust settled at once, and within moments the young woman was able to sweep a mound of dust and ash back into the fireplace. At that she glided serenely out of the room, curtseying deeply to the Curator as they passed in the doorway.

The man was grinning, a mischievous, twinkling grin which sat oddly on his professorial features. 'We deal in allegory here,' he said. (That did not make Christian feel any the less stupid; he was not sure he knew what allegory was.) 'The young lady's name is Gospel. This room represents the heart of a man who has never heard the Good News. When a person suddenly realises that there is

wickedness in the world, he searches his heart for ways to be rid of it. But of course the more he thinks about the wicked things he has done himself, mankind's long history of wickedness, and all the works needed to put the world to rights, he stirs up such a welter of daunting doubts that he often feels much worse than he did before. That's when he needs the Gospel – to prove to him that Good can and will always prevail over Bad. In the end.'

With a pang of humility, Christian realised that, far from earning supper by cleaning the exhibits, he had become an exhibit himself! 'I was sent here to learn, wasn't I?' he said. 'Show me more. I want to see more. I want to learn.'

'First you need a night's rest,' said the Curator kindly. 'Tomorrow you may see all the exhibits here in the Museum. And don't worry: tomorrow, all you need to do is watch.'

The Museum had a marvellous collection of automata – little moving models which, like puppets, performed the same little stories over and over again. Viewed through a peephole, they gave the impression of being lifesize. Like a child at a fairground, Christian ran from one machine to the next, but since the automata had no labels on them, and the puppets did not speak, he needed the Curator's help to understand just what he was seeing.

For instance, there were two children sitting at a table. One sat patiently, while the other wriggled and squirmed and cried and banged his spoon, demanding to be fed. By and by, a hatch opened and a plate of food was set down in front of the wriggler. He wolfed it down in a few spoonfuls, jeering at the other child, who had nothing and only sat calmly watching. Soon the food was gone.

Then the hatch was opened and food was set down in front of the quiet child, who ate it. But however much he ate, his plate filled up again. And the food looked *so delicious*, Christian would have liked to eat it himself!

'These children are Patience and Passion,' said the Curator. 'Passion wants happiness *now*, at once, instantly. He gets it, too, but of course it doesn't last. Patience waits for true happiness – the lasting kind which is never used up.'

The next model was of a fire – with real flames! A nasty swarm of little puppet men in red suits were pouring buckets of water on to the fire, and yet – amazing! – the fire kept burning.

'How is it done?' asked Christian, intrigued by the model-maker's ingenuity. The Curator led him round to the side of the machine, so that he could see how an oil can with a long nozzle was feeding the fire constantly with oil. 'Ah! Clever trick.'

'Not a trick at all,' said the Curator. 'An allegory. The fire represents all the good things a pilgrim can achieve when he sets his mind to it. The Enemy will try and stop him, but they don't realise what they are up against. The oil can, you see, is God. Now are you starting to understand, Mr Christian?'

In among the automata were glass cases, too, holding a variety of ancient objects – a tent-peg, a slingshot and five pebbles, the jawbone of an ass, a basket made of bullrushes, some locks of hair, a brick made without straw. . . Christian gave them only fleeting glances – museum exhibits can be deadly dull. And besides, there were no labels to explain what they were; Christian looked everywhere.

'The stories are all in your guidebook,' said the Curator, seeing him look. 'The greatest adventure stories in the world. The people who owned these things were all pilgrims themselves once; pilgrims after their own fashion.'

Another automaton showed a room with a door at one end guarded by a huge, ferocious-looking guard. Along either wall stood people with noisily knocking knees, not daring to approach the guarded door. Then in came a lad wearing a helmet and breastplate. Without waiting, he whipped out a short sword and rushed at the guard. The two little figurines jarred and jerked together, then the guard sat down hard – which made Christian laugh – and the lad leapt over him and darted out of the door.

'Don't tell me!' exclaimed Christian, starting to grasp the principle. 'The boy is Bravery. If you want to win through, you have to take your courage in both hands and just get on and do it.'

The Curator smiled and nodded. 'I see you do understand Allegory, after all.'

'Of course, *he* has armour. That's what I need,' said Christian wistfully. 'Anyone can be brave wearing a suit of armour.'

'Don't worry. You will pass the Armoury further down this road. In fact, you might stay there tonight if you make good progress today.'

Christian did not trouble to hide his disappointment. 'Oh. Are there no more exhibits to see, then?'

'Only one,' said the Curator. 'And some people choose not to look at it. It can be . . . unnerving.'

But Christian had been so delighted with the various peepshows that he thought nothing of rushing into the end room of the Museum, to the last exhibit of all. Inside, the room was totally black, and the door swung closed behind him, leaving the Curator outside.

As Christian's eyes grew accustomed to the dark, he could just make out pictures on the walls; the likeness of buildings rose up on all sides, and beyond them, mountains. 'Wh— It's my home town!' he exclaimed.

While he was still marvelling at the realism of the painting, these pictures began to move. The clouds on the ceiling gathered into a black maelstrom, and a moon rose up, blood-red. The mountains began to crumble, the ground to shake, and all around him the likeness of his town crashed into rubble amid a smell of sulphur.

Indeed, fire and molten lava poured out of the sky, splashing down like hot red porridge within a hair's breadth of Christian's head. Figures moved across the flickering sky, too – larger-than-life figures in red or in white, like two armies drawing up battle lines. All around him in the darkened room (which he had thought empty), there was a sound of running feet and screaming, and shapes brushed past Christian, fleeing in both directions, either towards the Red or the White. The white troops in the sky seemed, at the orders of their commander, to descend into the very town, cheered by some, while the rest fell down in cringing, pleading terror. Two doors, previously invisible, opened on to the room, one full of fire, like the mouth of a furnace, the other full of liquid light bubbling with inexpressibly sweet music. With a noise of breaking tidal waves, real cold water sluiced down on Christian's head, knocking him off his feet, stealing the breath out of him. And though no one draped Christian in chains or hauled him into the furnace, neither was he in time to reach the bright portcullis before it disappeared and became once more a brick wall, a plain, plastered wall.

Of the town where he had been born, not one brick or tile or beam remained, only the glistening likeness of a pearly pool.

Then daylight erased the room's last illusion, and in the doorway stood the Curator, waiting to usher Christian out of the Museum of Wonders.

'What you just saw . . .' he began to say.

'Don't tell me,' said Christian, gibbering with fright and cold, his knees like water and his heart as hammered as a smith's anvil. 'Don't tell me. I know what I saw. That was no allegory. That was the End of the World.'

Four

THE HILL

*In which Christian
sheds a great weight off
his shoulders and meets
some interlopers*

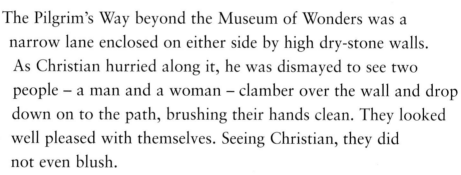

The Pilgrim's Way beyond the Museum of Wonders was a
narrow lane enclosed on either side by high dry-stone walls.
As Christian hurried along it, he was dismayed to see two
people – a man and a woman – clamber over the wall and drop
down on to the path, brushing their hands clean. They looked
well pleased with themselves. Seeing Christian, they did
not even blush.

'We came the quick way,' said the woman, with a shrug,
and introduced herself: Miss Stake.

'Only a fool would come in at the wicket gate,' said her
companion, Mr Smug. 'A person could get shot waiting there.'

'But you do have your scrolls, don't you?' queried Christian.
(Neither of them had a rucksack like his, and their hands
appeared to be empty.)

'We're in, aren't we?' Smug said. 'If we are in, we are in.
The great thing is to be in. Doesn't matter how you get there.'

The couple linked arms and set off along the straight-and-narrow
way, before Christian could repeat the Curator's last words of advice: '*Keep that
scroll of yours safe, now. Without that, you won't be allowed into the City of
Gold. That's your passport. And keep to the straight-and-narrow, no matter what!*'

The pair in front seemed so sure of themselves that Christian did not dare
argue with them. Besides, without rucksacks to weigh them down, they strode out

33

much faster than he, and reached the Hill long before he did.

The Hill in question was very steep, shaped rather like a skull, and covered in nettles and briars and thistles. At the foot of it, the lane appeared to split in three in the shadow of a signpost, one path running east round the base of the hill, one circling it to the west, the third climbing straight up. Both of the paths to right and left were smooth and broad and carpeted gold with primroses. A strange time of year for primroses, thought Christian.

Miss Stake and Smug began to quarrel about which way to go. While Christian was still too far off to hear exactly what they were saying, Miss Stake caught Smug a mighty slap on the cheek, stamped her foot, and stalked off to the east. Smug rubbed his cheek, muttered and mammered for a moment, then turned on his heel and went the other way – along the primrose path to the west.

When Christian reached the spot, he was able to read the signpost at the foot of the Hill.

'Perhaps Miss Stake could not read,' thought Christian. 'Perhaps Mr Smug was

very brave.' But not for one moment was Christian tempted to take the primrosy path himself: he had made that mistake once before, when Alec Smart tempted him to a short cut. This time he would do as he was told, and keep to the straight-and-narrow.

The further he went up the Hill, the better view he got of the surrounding countryside. For instance, he could see how the primrose path to the west petered out into sandy yellow flats, whereas the path Miss Stake had taken disappeared into thick, eerie woods wreathed in mists. 'I hope she'll be all right,' thought Christian uneasily. But of neither Miss Stake nor Mr Smug could he glimpse one rag, one bone, one hank of hair. It was as if they had disappeared without trace. 'Perhaps I'll meet up with them on the other side of the Hill,' thought Christian.

But he found something at the top of the Hill which put Smug and Stake completely out of mind.

Against a livid sky full of snarling clouds and fragments of rainbow, full of circling crows and doves, he gradually made out three trees.

No, they were not trees; they were man-made. They were wooden crosses, as terrible to contemplate as gallows are to a highwayman. Each was sunk into the ground and here and there rusty nails stuck out at haphazard angles. The wood around the nails was stained with blood.

To the top of the middle cross, a notice had been nailed which seemed to read *King of the Jews*.

No, now he looked at it squarely, it said nothing of the kind. It said *Light of the World* – or was it *The Truth and the Way*, or was it simply *The Door*? As the clouds scrolled by and the sunbeams caught it from different angles, the words changed, though the cross remained all too horribly the same. There was no mistaking it for anything other than it was – a brutal instrument of torture and execution on which a man had been nailed up to die of thirst or suffocation.

Christian's throat turned dry at the thought of it, his lungs too cramped to breathe. What if he had been there that day? What if he had seen it, that murderous cruelty, that unrightable wrong, that ghastly injustice committed under a hot afternoon sun? The thought was too much to hold in his head – like trying to hold hot metal between bare hands. It brought him to his knees.

Then, all of a sudden, with a noise like a horse shedding its saddle, the load on Christian's back fell off. It just fell off, and rolled down the far side of the hill.

He ran after it, as if it were full of his dearest belongings, before remembering how he had longed to be rid of it. He followed it as it bounced over gorse bushes and rabbit holes, over boulders and tree stumps. With a last jolt, it spun away into the mouth of a dark cave – a kind of burial cave with its rock door rolled aside.

Nervously, Christian went and peered inside the cave, but there was nothing to see – no rucksack, no body, no smell of death or decay. There were just a few strips of white cloth, and a faint smell of frankincense and myrrh.

After chasing the bag, and the rigours of climbing the Hill, Christian was very glad to come across a little arbour halfway down the other side. It was a delightful spot, with a bench and a fruit tree and a little drinking fountain specially provided to refresh pilgrims on their journey. The view was splendid. 'No sign, though, of Miss Stake or Mr Smug,' thought Christian.

Wasps were humming among the windfall apples, and the day was warm. Christian began to feel drowsy. He realised he had not slept soundly since the book was thrust into his hands. Even at the Museum of Wonders, he had had to sleep in his rucksack, unable to get it off. So, to the murmur of the wasps and the tinkling of water, Christian dozed off and slept, the sunlight purple on his eyelids, his hands resting on his knees. As he slept, his fingers relaxed and opened in the warmth, like the petals of a flower.

Five

SLEEPING LIONS

*In which Christian's
courage is put to the test
and he is obliged
to turn back*

Christian woke with a start. He had dreamed a garden, and in it Jesus leaning over him saying, *'What? Could you not stay awake one hour? Stay awake and pray!'*
But the voices which woke him were not in his dream.
'Did you see the size of it?' said one.

'Did you see the teeth?!' said another.
Two shrill creatures – a man and a woman – came pelting up the lane towards him, hands flailing, feet stumbling, yelping and whimpering like puppies newly stepped on.

'You're going the wrong way,' said Christian. 'The Golden City is that way.'

'You can keep your Golden City and everything in it!' said the white-faced man. 'We're going back!'

'That's right! You tell him, Tim!' shrilled the white-faced woman. 'Hardship is one thing but lions is another!'

'That's right, Miss Trust! You tell him! Great ravening lions just lying there waiting to eat up pilgrims like so many plates of meat! I'll do a lot – I'll put up with a lot – but nobody can make me feed myself to a pair of hungry lions!' And away they went over the Hill, Tim Id and Miss Trust, babbling and gibbering with fright.

They were not lying, either. Within half a mile, Christian could hear the roaring for himself, a throaty rumbling which echoed along the narrow lane like

approaching thunder. The dry stone walls on either side were high; there was no climbing over them to bypass whatever lay in his path. Christian either had to go on or turn back. He edged forward unhappily, wondering which way the wind was blowing and whether it would carry his scent to the lions.

Then he saw them – two of them – a lion on each side of the path, couchant, noses on their paws. At the sound of Christian's footsteps (or the smell of his sweat) they opened yellow eyes and folded back velvety lips to show a reef of yellow teeth.

All Christian's resolve, to dare all and to dare anything, evaporated at the sight of those teeth. He would be ripped to shreds by them if he went three yards more, and where was the virtue in that? What good did it do anybody? What grand purpose would be served by walking deliberately to certain death?

'Have faith,' said a voice.

What a time for his conscience to pipe up, thought Christian.

'Just have faith, Christian,' said the voice again, and he saw it was not his conscience speaking, but a young man watching him from the lane beyond the lions. He knew the boy, too. It was Faithful, who had pulled him out of the Great Bog.

Christian began to consider. Why would the King allow lions to prey on travellers using the Pilgrim's Way? Wouldn't he send hunters to shoot the beasts?

'They won't hurt you,' called Faithful. 'Just walk through!'

Of course, he might be lying.

Christian thought of the exhibit in the Museum of Wonders: of that little mannequin who had rushed at the guarded door when all the rest had stood by with knocking knees. All very well for him, thought Christian: he had armour on.

From beyond the lions, Faithful beckoned. It was all very well for him, too, thought Christian. *He* was on the far side.

There again, how had he got there?

Christian took two steps forward, and the lions rose to their feet, tongues lolling, mouths agape. Christian took two steps more, and the lions crouched for the spring. Christian closed his eyes, walked smartly forward . . .

. . . and felt the heat of furry bodies close to his skin, as the lions hurled themselves at him.

But just as their paws unsheathed steely claws, and their saliva splashed

the path at his feet, two stout metal chains clanked out to
their limit, and brought the cats up short. Though they
strained and bounded and roared, the chains kept
them *just short* of their prey, and Christian
walked through unscathed.

Satisfied Christian was safe,
Faithful turned and went on his way.
Christian ran to catch him up:
'Faithful! Faithful! It's me!' he called,
but the lions' roaring drowned out
his voice. 'Faithful! Wait! It's me,
Christian!'

Just as he caught the boy up, he
tripped and fell sprawling, knocking
Faithful off his feet too.

'Christian?'

'Faithful? It is you, isn't it? Oh, it's
so good to see a familiar face!'
The prospect of having company on
the journey was so wonderful that in
no time they felt as close as blood
brothers, talking and swapping
experiences.

It turned out that Faithful had lived
just a few doors down from Christian in
the City of Destruction. He had been there
when Ob Stinate and Mr Bendy had returned
after deciding not to travel with Christian.

'When Bendy came back to town,' Faithful
recounted, 'he went about bad-mouthing you,
calling you a madman and a trickster. But no one
listened. Some people said he was a coward
because he had given up at the first hurdle. Some
said he was a coward to have run off in the first place! His business colleagues

said *they* couldn't trust him any more to make a decision without changing his mind. His wife couldn't forgive him for leaving without a word. When I left town, he had locked himself in his attic and wouldn't come out for anything: said he didn't dare.'

Naturally, Christian asked after his own parents and was overjoyed to hear that they, too, were planning to set out soon for the City of Gold. 'It wasn't until you left that they realised you really meant what you said,' Faithful explained.

Just then, the Armoury came into sight – a dour, forbidding building, but as brilliant with lighted windows as the Museum had been. Faithful pulled out his scroll from his jacket, in readiness to present it to the porter. Christian, too, felt for his.

'Oh no. Oh no, no, no, no, no,' he whispered, his eyes filling with instant tears. 'I'm a fool and a villain. I'm an oaf and a half-wit.'

'Whatever's the matter?' asked Faithful.

But Christian had already started back along the path, running flat out, head forward, eyes scouring the ground. 'I've only gone and dropped it!' he called over his shoulder. 'You'll have to go on without me! I've only gone and lost my scroll!'

Back he went, along the darkening lane, between the lions, who once more

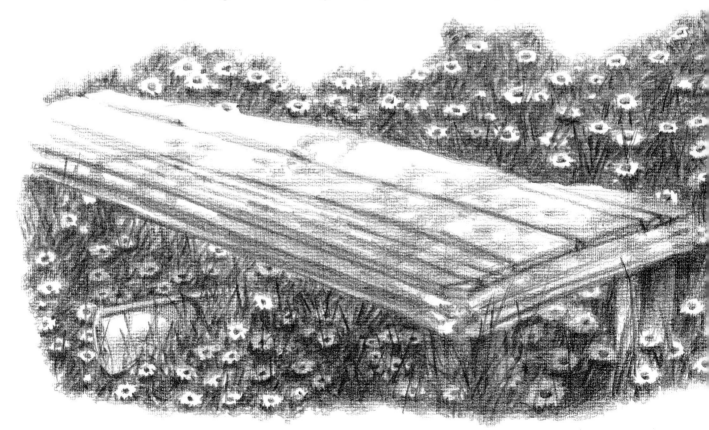

bounded to the full extent of their chains. Christian hardly even saw them; his eyes were so intently sweeping the ground for a sight of his precious scroll. Without it he could never enter the Golden City, and with the daylight fading, such a small thing would soon be hidden by darkness. Perhaps even now a rat in some ditch was gnawing on his priceless parchment.

The Hill loomed up over him, the three crosses on its crest lost against the darkening sky. Hands down, knees bent, he scrabbled up towards the arbour with its tinkling fountain.

He sank his arm up to the shoulder in the vine and fumbled about. He looked below the fruit tree, and on the ledges of the fountain. Then he got down on his knees, and wormed in under the bench where he had slept.

There it lay, pale in the darkness, cool under his hand. He hugged it to him

like a winner's trophy, and danced a little hopping dance there under the tree.

'What a fool I was to fall asleep!' he laughed up at the anxious moon. 'Preacher told me not to fall asleep! To be watchful and keep awake! Never again! I'll never sleep again!' No one witnessed this vow but the rolling silver moon floating over silvery Lucre Hill, and the startled lions roaring themselves hoarse as their collars chafed their thick manes.

Within a couple of hours, Christian was back at the Armoury door, knocking for all his might, but hardly daring to hope that anyone would open up at this late hour. The countryside was infested with bandits and villains; why should law-abiding people open to a knocking in the night?

A small shutter slid back in the door, and a small, freckled nose protruded through it. 'You're very late,' said a woman's voice. 'We were starting to worry about you.'

Six

APOLLYON

In which Christian is given a suit of armour, and finds great need of it

Christian had expected the Armoury to be in the charge of some battle-hardened war veteran. But it proved to be the home of three quiet and amiable girls: Prudence, Patience and Charity. They brought Christian a delicious supper of bread and wine, then showed him up to a bedroom where Faithful already lay sleeping: a room called Peace. In that room, the pilgrims slept the deepest, most delectable sleep they had ever enjoyed. Sometimes sleeping is perfectly right, you see.

In the morning, the women took them to the workshop, and pulled, from amid heaps of brightly shining equipage, two breastplates, helmets, swords and shields, as well as two pairs of boots with soles of some indestructible substance.

'However far your journey takes you, at least your boots will never wear out!' said the girls, laughing. 'Now put on your armour – the sword-belt of Truth, the breast-plate of Righteousness, the shield of Faith, the helmet of Salvation and the sword of the Spirit.'

Christian did all this, then began nosing about amid the greaves and bucklers and sheaths and maces. 'What are you looking for?' asked Charity.

'A backplate – to cover my back,' said Christian, upsetting a stack of pikes.

'If you turn your back on the Enemy, you are lost anyway,' said Prudence sternly. 'We don't issue backplates.'

45

But Christian was not unduly put out. He had just caught sight of himself in the windowglass – the bright casque on his head, the shining thrust of his breastplate, the shield with its blood-red cross. 'I look just like Saint George,' he thought, squaring his shoulders. 'I'm a footsoldier of the King! What better fate could a man come to?'

The two friends felt invulnerable as they set off from the Armoury – this time across a green and pleasant plain. They believed themselves ready for any encounter with the Enemy. Christian whistled fitfully between his teeth.

Of course, Faithful had done rather better than he had, he mused. Faithful had not lost his scroll, fallen in the Bog or been misled by Alec Smart. *And* he had passed by the lions without knowing about the chains fastening them. In fact, he felt moved to say out loud, 'This pilgrimage has been plain sailing for you, hasn't it, Faithful?'

'Who, me?' Faithful looked amazed, then burst out laughing. 'Plain sailing? If you only knew how close I came to running aground!'

Faithful had not met Alec Smart, or Smug or Miss Trust during the early part of his journey. But he had met an old man on the Pilgrim's Way, who had said to him: 'I've had my eye on you, young man. You conduct yourself very creditably. I'm impressed.' In fact, the old man had taken such a shine to Faithful that he offered him a job. 'What kind of job?' asked Faithful, pleasantly taken aback.

'Estate manager. Mine's a fine big estate, though I say it myself. It's the tragedy of my life that I have no son to help me run it. Only three lovely daughters. Come and see for yourself, why don't you? I'd be honoured to have a boy like you as a guest under my roof!'

Faithful thought it could do no harm, just to go and see.

The old man was not exaggerating. His estates were huge, with orange groves, vineyards, sheep-pens and herds of cattle. Rambling roses covered the house, and there were fishponds in the garden. The three daughters (and Faithful was a great connoisseur of beautiful girls) were the loveliest he had ever laid eyes on. Over dinner he could hardly take his eyes off them. Black-haired, blonde and redhead, they returned his stare with shy but delighted smiles, glancing up coyly through their top lashes, and jumping up to refill his cup. Surprisingly often, their hips brushed against him as they passed his chair.

Faithful began daydreaming. Perhaps, if he stayed, it was not impossible that he might (when he had got to know them, of course) just *might* win the love of one of these breathtaking girls!

'My daughters seem to find you as agreeable as I do,' said the old man later, as they walked in the garden. 'If you do decide to stay, it would rejoice my heart to have you for my son-in-law.'

'O-ho! I should hardly know which of your lovely daughters to choose!' laughed Faithful. 'They are all so . . .'

'Oh, marry all three, if you have a mind to, my boy! It's the custom in these parts. That way I would gain a son, a manager and an heir all at one stroke. Nothing could please me more.'

Now who wouldn't give such an offer serious consideration? Faithful promised to sleep on it, and to give his answer in the morning.

Fortunately, Faithful was in the habit of saying his prayers each night before getting into bed. This night of all nights, he had a great deal to pray about. Since the moon was full, he went and sat on his bedroom windowsill, overlooking the moonlit garden. Clasping his hands, he lowered his head in meditation.

When he heard the door of his room open, he almost called out a greeting. Luckily, he heard, in the nick of time, the unmistakable clanking of chain links, and the shadow cast by the moon against the bedroom wall showed a pair of

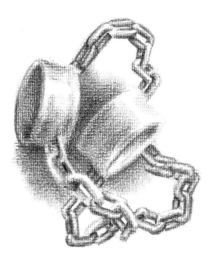

manacles dangling from a fist. The figures of three women, each carrying candles, followed their father's into the room, whispering, 'Bind him, Father, and quick! This one will fetch a good price.'

Down from the sill, into the shadowy garden, jumped Faithful. He knew now what the old man's riches were founded on: *slavery!*

'He lures young men into his house, with promises of love and riches, only to make slaves of them!' Faithful told Christian, as the Armoury passed finally out of sight behind them. 'Either he forces them to till all those lush acres of his, or he sells them into captivity abroad, rowing galleys or mining guano. It was a narrow escape, I can tell you! I'll probably never know for certain what my answer would have been to his offer. I think I was just about ready to give up my pilgrimage altogether.'

Faithful could not quite understand why Christian looked so *pleased* by this sad story of temptation and trickery. He did not realise how much better Christian felt, to know that he was not the only one who had made mistakes along the way.

'In fact, all in all, I've done pretty well to get this far,' Christian was thinking to himself. 'Here I am, cutting a dash in the Armour of Salvation, with the Great Bog and the Hill behind me, my scroll safe in my pocket, and the Golden City practically in sight.'

He heard Faithful behind him give a strangled cry, but with his ears covered by the helmet of Salvation, Christian mistook it for a sneeze. When Faithful passed him, running, he admired the boy's energy, but he did not think to start running himself.

When, at last, he saw the monster loping towards him across the plain, he found it was too late to run, because his legs would not obey him.

The monster had wings like a dragon, feet like a bear, and the mouth of a lion. It was covered, from its snarling snout to its mace-like tail, in shining fish scales, and fire and smoke issued out of its navel with a noise like a blacksmith's bellows.

'*STAND STILL, PETTY SUBJECT!*' roared the monster. '*STAND STILL AND NAME YOURSELF! ARE YOU NOT SOME RUNAWAY SLAVE OF MINE?*'

Christian stood stock still. Although Faithful was also in plain view, running for his life, the monster paid him no attention; it seemed interested only in Christian, bestriding the path ahead of him, barring his way forwards.

'It's true that once upon a time I used to serve a master something like you,' said Christian, in a small, quailing voice. 'But my name is Christian now, and my new master is the King of this land!'

The monster tossed its hideous head and pawed the ground. 'Exactly. As I said. My subject. I am Apollyon. This land is mine. I rule it. Therefore anyone inside its borders is my subject.'

Christian tried to catch his breath – to keep it from deserting him in little sobs of fright. 'Then I must get on my way out of your land, sir, as fast as my legs will carry me. Because I am bound for the City of Gold!'

At the mention of the City, Apollyon shuddered a little, and his scales dimmed, but he made a kind of purring noise and drew in his claws, smiling with all his ivory teeth. 'A wise king values his subjects and wants to keep them at his right hand. Don't go. Stay and serve ME.'

'I don't like the wages you pay, or the job prospects,' said Christian, starting to recover himself.

'Then I will pay you better. Indeed, I may even share with you some of my power. What do you say?'

Christian's fingers closed round his sword hilt. 'I say that I fight now under a different banner, and that you have no power against the forces of my King!'

'Oh, but consider, Christian,' sneered Apollyon, abandoning bribery in favour of contempt. 'Consider what a *failure* you have been as a pilgrim. What are your chances of winning through to the end? You who fall into bogs; you who fall asleep when you should be praying; you who forget the instructions of your commander.'

'All that's true,' said Christian. 'But my new King forgives me, and for that I will never leave his service!'

The heat within Apollyon seethed and bubbled, and his scales clicked. 'You deserted *me*, didn't you?' jeered Apollyon. His logic was crushing. 'And for that I will *spill your soul.*'

Christian knew there was nothing left but to unsheath his sword and fight the Beast until his last breath.

Apollyon came down on him like a bolt of lightning. Snatching handfuls of fire from its hair and stomach, and shaping them into darts, it hurled the darts at Christian, who flung up his shield and deflected the fire. Apollyon threw darts with both paws then – raining them thick and fast on the pilgrim. One struck his foot and made him stumble, another his hand, so that his sword went spinning away through the air. A third dart struck Christian on the brow, and he went down, pole-axed, clutching his head. Darkness welled up in his brain, threatening to swallow him.

Then Apollyon fell on him like volcanic lava, gripping his throat and banging his head on the ground till the helmet of Salvation rolled away, bent and bowed. He could barely draw breath for the weight of the monster on his chest, and the smell of sulphur was suffocating. Piece by piece, his armour was stripped away, like the bark flayed off a tree.

But a man fighting destruction can muster the strength of ten, and Christian fought without thought for the pain or the odds against him. For an hour they rolled and tussled, the fire of Apollyon's hair setting light to the plain, and Christian's blood quenching it. For an hour, and then another, they wrestled and battled, hand-to-hand, face to muzzle, and all the while Christian grew weaker, because of the wounds the darts had made on him. At last Apollyon sat back on his haunches, eyed Christian up and down with a scornful grin, and lifted a paw to deal the last crushing blow that would rip out Christian's heart.

At that instant, Christian flung out an arm; his fingertips found the hilt of his lost sword, and he swung it inwards and upwards. 'Too soon to rejoice, Apollyon!' he gasped, and made his thrust, piercing the monstrous belly just below the ribs.

Apollyon made no sound, uttered no cry. His grinning jowls simply uncreased, and the fire of his eyes cooled to a blue glimmer. The great leathery dragon wings, which all this while had hung folded down his back, suddenly unfurled, blotting out Christian's sunlight, and Apollyon rose into the air, one paw to his wounded belly. On a sulphurous wind of his wings' making, he soared into the sky, diminishing to the size of a raven, flapping away over the landscape. Christian fell back, his strength exhausted. He did not see Faithful come pelting back across the plain; did not see from which tree his friend plucked the leaves with which he salved Christian's wounds.

'Leaves from the Tree of Life,' said Faithful, as Christian finally opened his eyes.

'Yes, but it took the hands of a friend to bring them.'

'You were magnificent,' said Faithful.

But Christian knew better than to glory in his victory over Apollyon. 'The Beast was drawn to the smell of pride on me,' he said. 'My wounds are no more than I deserved. I don't mean to let him smell me out a second time.'

They rested and recuperated under the shade of the Tree of Life – and had sat there a long while before they realised someone was sitting on the other side of the same tree trunk. He came ducking into view now under a low branch, and they instantly recognised the silvery hair, the flat clerical hat, the white collar tabs at the throat of his sombre black coat.

'*Preacher!*'

'You have done well,' said Preacher, fixing them equally with his penetrating stare. (It felt as if he were able to see through them to some inner page where all they had seen and done was written large.) 'Both of you have done very well. Now it is time for one of you to end his journey and one to go on.'

They protested: said they had decided to stick together, to keep each other company all the way to the City of Gold. But he waved aside their protests of friendship and undying comradeship. 'You are coming to a place full of trouble and danger. One of you will be asked to pay the fare and speed ahead by the only quick route to the Golden City.' Both pilgrims began feeling for their purses, anxious because they had brought so little money, had very little left for fares . . . But Preacher shook his head. 'You can both of you muster the price, I assure you. This particular fare is paid in blood . . . So rise up, pilgrims! The time has come for one of you to die.'

Seven

VANITY FAIR

In which everything is for sale, and the pilgrims are asked to pay the price

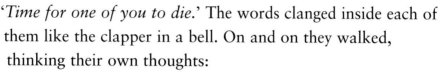

'Time for one of you to die.' The words clanged inside each of them like the clapper in a bell. On and on they walked, thinking their own thoughts:

'Will it be me?'

'Will it be him?'

Maybe you think each wished death on the other, hoping to be spared. But no. A delicious excitement burned hot inside them, a scalding exhilaration. No more travelling! No more hardships! To leap with a single bound into the Celestial City! Surely that would be best. That would be the heroic way!

'Let it be me,' Christian was thinking.

'Let it be me,' thought Faithful.

And they were so absorbed that, before they realised it, they were in among the tents and booths of a gigantic fairground – a huge, sprawling market. The road went directly through it.

For five thousand years, Vanity Fair has thrived and grown bigger. There is no bypassing it. When it was founded, all those years ago, the instigator made very sure to site it right on the Pilgrim's Way. Most of its traders, most of its customers were pilgrims once. Somehow they just never got any further along the road than this: Vanity Fair.

The place is one huge hugger-mugger confusion of stalls, carts and hand-barrows, colourful with brightly striped awnings and fluttering bunting. A few dark caravans sell their wares out of open back doors. Hawkers and hustlers, with trays full of trinkets slung round their necks, wander up and down, touting for trade. Night and day the fair never falls silent, each barrow-boy trying to shout down his rivals, no one ever packing up to go home, no opportunity to clear the litter that blows along the lanes and midway. There is no shortage of customers, and something to tempt everyone . . .

Christian and Faithful could not help but see, as they walked down the midway, just what extraordinary goods were for sale. Some stalls were selling the sort of things you would expect: cones of sweets, tawdry twinkling jewellery, pork from a pig roast, china and hardware.

'Clothes! Pretty clothes! All the latest fashions! Come and try on the pretty clothes!'

Meats and sweetmeats. Bread and sweetbreads. Persian carpets and Irish linen. Chinese silk, African violets and fine French wines. Every country in the world is represented at Vanity Fair.

But some were selling much stranger things.

'Wives for sale! Lovely elegant wives! How can you do without one? Trade in the old one for a new!'

'Gold! Silver! Pearls! Cheap! Cheap! Cheap!'

'Have your portrait painted! Have your statue carved and set up in a public place. You, sir! Fame, sir! And it's yours for the asking!'

'Land for sale! Acres and acres! Mountains and lakes! Oceans and rivers! How about you, sir. You look like a volcano man, to me! Or perhaps a plantation?'

A man waving a sword pointed it at Faithful. 'Sir! Sir! Yes, you, sir! A knighthood for you, sir? Shall I dub you a knight, sir, tonight, sir? When will you get a better offer? Or perhaps you're a sports-man. What about a trophy? A laurel wreath?

The victor ludorum!'

In addition to the goods, every booth in Vanity Fair was up for sale, the lanes full of carts and baggage as people moved continuously to bigger and better pitches. There were stands, too, where a pilgrim could try his luck – enter a lottery, shoot dice, or shy a ball at a coconut. In a boxing ring, a pugilist shouted out a challenge to all-comers, and punched at the shadows.

A man was selling slaves from a big cage – as if they were songbirds. 'Be the envy of your neighbours! Take life easy, with a maid or a manservant!'

'You, sir!' brayed a costermonger to Christian. 'Can I offer you a job?'

'Doing what?' said Christian, caught unawares.

'What do you fancy? A banker? A captain? A bishop? Everything has a price. If you've got the money, son, I can make you a president!'

But though Vanity Fair sold every worldly thing hearts have ever desired, neither Christian nor Faithful were tempted. They did not make a single purchase. Their hearts were set on the treasures of the Celestial City, and that made everything here seem worthless and tawdry – a needless distraction, and an extra load to carry as well, over the long miles ahead. They tried not even to look at the goods on sale, keeping their eyes averted.

The din, which had been loud enough when they first entered the fairground, gradually grew louder the further they went. They very soon noticed that the shouting now was directed at them.

'Look at these two, turning up their noses at our stock! Who do they think they are?'

'Too mean to spend their money, that's what!'

'Certainly look in need of a new suit of clothes!'

'They lower the tone of the place, the ragamuffins!' One came and thrust his face up against Faithful's, ferocious in his desire to make a sale. 'All right,

Mr High-and-Mighty Scarecrow. What *will* you buy?'

Faithful gave a wry smile. 'I don't think you would have anything I'm after,' he said, and made to step round the man. But the costermonger pushed him in the chest. A crowd began to gather round. Fast, sleek horses for sale in a nearby corral, stamped and rolled their eyes.

'What's it to you if we don't choose to buy?' asked Christian reasonably. 'There seem to be plenty of others who will.'

But the barrow-boys and fishwives, the roustabouts, estate agents and house dealers, and the man with the sword were incensed. 'Suppose they think they're *better* than us!' shrieked a fishwife. 'Well, what *do* they want, exactly?'

Faithful glanced at Christian. Preacher had warned them they would meet trouble, danger – Death, even – in Vanity Fair. 'I'll buy a basket of Truth, if you have it,' he said, in a flurry of daring.

For a moment the crowd fell back. Some even rushed to their stalls and stock-books to see if they had any Truth for sale. They had racing pigeons in baskets, news-sheets, legal parchments sealed up with wax. . . . Others saw at once that Faithful was making fun of them, belittling their occupation, slighting their life's work. They laid hold of both pilgrims by the hair, manhandled them on to a barrow, and ran with them through the bumpy fairground.

At the back of the fair stood a row of animal cages on wheels. Once they had housed rare animals with valuable fur, and birds bred for the beauty of their feathers. But most of the species had become extinct, and so the cages stood empty. Into one of these the fairground people bundled Christian and Faithful, kicking and punching them, even though they put up no kind of struggle.

Hysterical with rage, a couple of hucksters put their shoulders to the cage and began to push it through the fair, bawling out that these rogues had spurned the great Vanity Fair. Up and down the midway they pushed the cage until, worn out, they stopped it amid noisy, gawping crowds. Some poked sticks through the bars, and said that hanging was too good for such unnatural misers; hooligans, they were, and anarchists.

One bright-faced young woman, though, with raised eyebrows and a look of permanent astonishment, watched more carefully how Christian and Faithful conducted themselves. The pilgrims sat cross-legged in their cage and weathered the insults peaceably, without retaliating. When the swearing, cursing bullies

paused for breath, this onlooker quietly ventured the opinion that 'the two did not look much like hooligans to her'.

'You're right,' said another. 'Seems to me there are cheats hereabouts who deserve locking up more than these two. Harmless fools, that's all they are. There are worse crimes than not buying.'

'Like giving short change.'

'And selling shoddy goods!'

'Is that remark a snipe at me?' demanded a fishwife.

'Well, if the cap fits . . .'

A jostling and shoving broke out among the crowd, and for a moment Christian and Faithful were forgotten, as stallholders and hucksters argued and scrimmaged among themselves. Then a loud, authoritative voice called for silence, and the fair's site manager shouldered his way through to the cage. 'What's going on here?' he demanded to know.

'These two pilgrims . . .'

'. . . vagrants! Scarecrows!'

'. . . wouldn't buy . . .'

'. . . wouldn't even look . . .'

'. . . asked for a basket of Truth . . .'

'. . . think they're too good for the likes of us!'

The site manager held up his hands. 'Then they shall be tried tomorrow, for disturbing the peace! Now, everyone get back to your stalls and booths, will you? Your customers are waiting!'

The crowd dispersed – all but the bright-faced girl with yellow hair and high eyebrows, who sat down at a distance and seemed to be watching, just watching. It was getting late. Inside the cage-on-wheels, Christian and Faithful scrabbled together the dirty straw into a heap, said their prayers, and bedded down as best they could in such an uncomfortable cell. The fair grew dark, though loud music continued to thump at a distance, and voices went on calling.

'Nice little maid for sale!'

'Buy yourself an earldom!'

'Win an ox!'

The pilgrims heard none of it. They heard only the voice of Preacher in their heads, saying, 'It is time for one of you to pay the price. It is time for one of you to die.'

The excitement of it was still in their stomachs, but now it had turned to a sour acid which burned as they lay awake.

'Will it be you?'

'Will it be me?'

Christian was no longer sure he wanted to buy fast passage to the Celestial City if it meant . . . if it meant . . .

In the morning, a makeshift courtroom was put together out of flat-carts and trestle tables. There were jury, witnesses and a prosecution. The Judge was the site manager of the fair, wearing a wig he had bought from the wig-stall and a robe he had bought second-hand.

The salesman with the sword accused Faithful and Christian of causing a disturbance, of belittling the excellence of Vanity Fair by not looking, not buying, not caring a ripe fig about his lovely knighthoods.

The clothes-seller said that their very appearance condemned them: '. . . ragged, odd-looking, *different*.' He rucked his top lip as he testified, spitting out the words like grape pips.

A fishwife testified that the two had caused an affray, and showed her black eye in evidence.

'Did one of the prisoners give you that?' asked the Judge.

'Nay, but they were the reason why we was fighting!' she testified.

The Judge's face grew steadily blacker beneath his powdered wig. 'What else? What else? Let's hear it all, all the crimes these good-for-nothing rascals have committed in this our fairest of fairs.'

'Unfairest, you mean,' said a voice, and the bright-faced girl with the high brows stood up. She looked dishevelled after her night in the open, and scared too. 'May I speak a word in defence of the prisoners?' she asked.

'Just one? Oh well . . . if you must. Take the stand, if you must, Miss . . . whoever-you-are.'

'Hopeful is my name,' said the bright-faced girl. 'I was there yesterday when these two arrived, and it seemed to me that they did nothing wrong.' She blushed and kept nervously ducking her head, gripping the rail of the witness box which was an old handbarrow. 'They were dignified and they never raised their voices. They didn't sneer or criticise – though God knows, there's enough to criticise in Vanity Fair!' (An angry murmur rippled round the courtroom.) 'They simply didn't choose to buy . . . No, no, even that's not true!' she corrected herself. 'That one there offered to buy a basket of Truth, if we had any to sell. But of course it wasn't there to buy. I've looked myself, and I know. It isn't for the having. Not in Vanity Fair.'

Hopeful stood down. The Judge's face was darker than ever. His black silk seethed and boiled round him, so that he looked like a brute beast struggling in a tar-pit.

'Offered to buy the *Truth*?' he hissed between clenched teeth. 'Well, I can serve you with that, villain! The truth is that you are a dissenter and a trouble-maker, a whipper-up of discontent, a cloud in our sunny skies, a cat among our pigeons! Let the prisoner called Faithful pay the price for disturbing the peace of Vanity Fair!' He covered his head with a piece of black cloth. 'Death to Faithful and let his death be as miserable as he!'

Christian reached out to grasp his friend's hand, but the mob dragged their fingers apart, and swept Faithful away on a tide of swearing, abuse and hatred. Christian gripped the bars of his cage and shook them, roaring for justice, for mercy, for a retrial. But his voice was soon the only one left crying in the empty midway, as the people of Vanity Fair carried Faithful away to execution.

He heard screaming, but did not cover his ears, did not allow himself to cover his ears. He owed that much to Faithful. Instead, he pressed his hands together in prayer, and prayed that Faithful should not suffer too terribly before blessed Death brought him peace and an end to all his pain.

But his prayers became all muddled with anxiety for himself. Christian wondered whether the mob would come back for him, when they had finished with Faithful. His eagerness to die seeped away through the palms of his hands. In terror, he hurled himself at the door of the cage.

And, to his astonishment, he found that the mob had forgotten to lock the cage again. The door swung open and dumped him on his face in the dirt.

Mercifully, the screaming had stopped. Even the music had fallen quiet. Christian dried his eyes with the heel of his hand and stood up. Stumbling over the guy ropes of a dozen silent fairground booths, he found himself on the edge of some rough, open ground. Faithful's body lay there, sprawled in the trampled mud, like a rag doll lost and forgotten. His murderers had all moved away.

At that moment, a hand fell on Christian's shoulder; his heart banged against his ribs. But the hand belonged to Hopeful, the bright-faced girl who had spoken up for them in court.

'I'll keep you company on the journey,' said Hopeful. 'If you want me to.'

Christian nodded. He was grateful. The loneliness inside him just then was bigger than an empty cupboard. 'Did Faithful – did my friend say anything before he died?' he asked.

'Only one thing,' said Hopeful. 'He said how Jesus Christ walked through Vanity Fair Himself, once upon a time. And He bought nothing either. That's no more nor less than the Truth.'

All at once, there was a thunder of hooves and a flash, as of sunlight off a mirror. A chariot, driven by a man in white and pulled by creamy horses, came hurtling through the narrow passageways of the crowded fair. Tents billowed, but none collapsed, none of the barrows were overturned, despite the charioteer's breakneck speed. No one jumped out of the way, either. In fact, the hucksters did not even appear to notice this reckless hurtling arrival. It seemed that Faithful's poor tormented body must be mangled once more, this time by the chariot's wheels, and Christian almost darted out of hiding to try and drag it clear.

But then the charioteer reined in his horses a hand's span from Faithful's head, and jumped nimbly down. He took hold of Faithful's bloody hand and, for a wild moment, Christian thought his friend must not have died after all!

But Faithful's shoes, as he stepped aboard the chariot, made no sound, and the sunlight passed directly through his clothing, through his form. He was no sooner standing in the chariot than the creamy horses sprang into a gallop again and, finding purchase in the sunny air, climbed steeply into the morning sky.

Vanity Fair is not so very far from the Celestial City, as the crow flies. At such speed and aboard such a vehicle, Faithful stood every chance of reaching his destination by sunset.

'Did you see that?' said Christian in a breathless whisper.

'I saw something. I'm not sure. My eyes are not good,' said Hopeful.

They walked together out of Vanity Fair.

'Are we the only people, then, who prize our journey more than all those . . . *baubles*?' said Christian, though he was only thinking aloud.

'No,' said Hopeful. 'Others will follow, when they can tear themselves away. You and your friend made a lot of people think today – good people who were pilgrims once, but gave up – got sidetracked, got blinded to their visions by the razzle-dazzle of this place. I'd be surprised if others didn't follow on behind us in a few days.'

At the edge of the fairground, Christian shaded his eyes and tried to make out the flying shape of Faithful's chariot against the brightness of the sky. But it was already too far ahead to be seen, or else it was hidden by the scrolling clouds and the wildly waving treetops.

'Keep a place for me, Faithful,' said Christian under his breath. 'And remember me, dear friend, next time we meet.'

Eight

FILTHY LUCRE

*In which Hopeful is
dazzled and Christian
takes her to look over
the brink*

At first they were delighted when fellow pilgrims Natter
Jack and Owen Ends caught them up on the road. Natter
held out the promise of a good lively discussion, and
Owen Ends seemed such a very *religious* man.

But then Natter Jack began to talk . . . and talked . . .
and talked. He talked about whether Christians should use
their right hand or their left; about whether Christians
should eat fish on Fridays or read books on Sundays; about
how many children they should have and which language
the angels speak. He talked about the Past and the Future,
his wife's past and his children's future. He talked about
every subject known to man or woman or dog. And he
never once stopped to listen or think or (it seemed) even
to draw breath. He simply liked to talk.

Christian did learn one useful thing from him, though.
He learned the value of silence – of peace and calm and
companionable quiet; of walking along with only the birdsong for accompaniment,
and only thought to occupy the mind.

To give him his due, Natter Jack knew the contents of Christian's guidebook
from cover to cover, and could quote whole pages at a time. He never offered an
opinion on what he had read there, but stated his own opinions as if they were

67

absolute scientific fact. Nothing could dent his conviction that he knew everything worth knowing about the King, the Golden City, the Pilgrim's Way. As they topped each hill, he would look around him and say, 'Ah yes, yes,' as if he had known what to expect all along.

The stridency of his voice was like cymbals being clashed in their ears, and when – finally – Natter Jack took offence (because Christian dared to disagree with him) and stalked away in a huff, they offered up heartfelt thanks that he had gone.

'I hear he never did anyone a favour in his life,' said Hopeful.

'I doubt he ever stopped talking long enough for anybody to ask one,' said Christian, and that set them both off laughing. They felt a little ashamed of themselves (as they leaned against each other hooting and wiping their eyes) for criticising another pilgrim behind his back.

Mr Ends was a different matter altogether. Somehow he did not move Christian to laughter – only to a deeply uncomfortable feeling, as if a handful of ice were sliding down inside his shirt. Christian told himself he was simply giving in to envy, because Owen Ends seemed to have met with no hardship, no fear, no difficulty on his own, long pilgrimage.

'Hardships? Never! It's simply the best life in the world!' Ends exclaimed in his rich, orator's voice. 'On the contrary, it's been the making of me!'

'How's that?' asked Hopeful, hoping to learn from this handsome and distinguished-looking man.

'Well, it stands to reason: nobody likes a rascal, do they? Take women! You women like a man you can trust; a man of delicate feelings and good character. Aren't I right? Why, I've had women simply *flocking* round me since I gave up my old, sinful life. I've had the pick of them! Chose myself the richest of the lot, and now I move among high society. Take business! Colleagues, investors, dealers – they all know they can trust a *religious* man not to run off with their money, don't they? So I get easier credit, better contracts, less trouble from accountants and tax men . . . And you don't get rogues being elected to positions of power, I mean *do* you? Me, I've been mayor three times, I've sat on the Parish Council and the District Council and the County Council, two boards of governors, four Charity Commissions . . . I tell you, religious respectability opens the door to all manner of high places. How else do you think I became a Justice of the Peace? And I think I can safely expect a knighthood before the year's out.'

There was no faulting his logic, and the others had only to look at Owen Ends' otter-skin coat and braided tricorn hat to see that he was telling the truth about his successes.

And yet Hopeful shot an anxious glance in Christian's direction, to see if he could calm her unease. Should she in fact *admire* this pillar of society, this eminent citizen? Why, then, did she not?

'Do you believe in it, though?' Christian asked Mr Ends.

'Believe in what?'

'All of it. Your religion. Religion. This religion of ours.'

'*Believe in it?*' said Mr Ends, bewildered. 'I act on it, don't I? Oh, believe me, I don't put a foot wrong! Never. A man in my position can't afford to. Me, I play by the rules. You can't win this game unless you put your heart and soul into it.'

Then it was Christian's turn to glance across at Hopeful: perhaps his young friend could see the flaw in the argument, the fly in the ointment of the oh-so-smooth Mr Owen Ends.

Suddenly, a noise of clattering machinery came to them on the wind and plumes of dust rose above the crest of a ragged hill, off to one side of the path. At the roadside stood a man in a waistcoat of fabulous ornateness, embroidered with silver wire. He was beckoning eagerly. 'Come on! Come and see! We've just struck a new seam!

There's not a minute to lose!'

'Take care, Hopeful,' said Christian under his breath. 'This may be some kind of a trap.' Then he nodded a greeting to the man in the waistcoat, and asked, 'What hill is that?'

'That, sir? That is Lucre Hill – site of the greatest silver mine in the world! I'm Chief Engineer there. Pluto's the name, Pluto Crat. There's so much high-grade silver in that mine, man, that a few hours' digging can make a man rich for the rest of his days!'

'Ah! Silver,' said Christian calmly. 'I regret, we are on a very important journey. I'm afraid we cannot spare the time for a visit.'

But Hopeful was clearly excited. 'I've never seen a silver mine, Christian.

Couldn't we just go and look?'

'Yes, Christian,' said Owen Ends. 'Where's the harm in going to look? Consider what *good* a man could achieve with a single sackful of silver!'

'Yes, Christian!' said Hopeful, who had never had two pennies to call her own. 'Imagine! Imagine being able to build a hospital for injured pilgrims – or somewhere for the homeless to shelter from the cold! Or a school for street children in Vanity Fair!' In her enthusiasm, she dragged Christian after her, following the man in the embroidered waistcoat. Owen Ends was also eager to see the silver mine, and was already walking arm-in-arm with Pluto Crat, discussing the nature of the mining operation.

'Hopeful, wait!' said Christian, digging in his heels. 'At least look before you leap! At least spy out the land, won't you? Please, Hopeful. Just for my sake.'

Hopeful was adamant that she was not abandoning her pilgrimage – would never abandon her pilgrimage. She simply wanted to spend half a day at the silver mine furnishing herself with enough money to last the journey, and just possibly enough to do some good in the world. But she allowed Christian to hold her back, while Pluto Crat and Owen Ends went on ahead.

'Up there,' said Christian, pointing. 'From up there we can see this famous mine for ourselves before you decide whether you want to visit it.'

Hopeful could not understand his caution, but she agreed, even so, and they scrambled up the side of the hill, until they reached a ridge to the east of the dust and noise which was Lucre Silver Mine.

They found, to their consternation, that the whole other side of the hill had been sliced away, so as to drop sheer down, flat as a wall: Lucre Hill now consisted of a beetling cliff of astounding height, pitted and cratered by explosions and quarrying. Whole armies of men teemed like ants over the rockface, roped together in teams, each man hacking at the cliff with picks or mallets, showering down shards on the men below as they, too, scrabbled for the ore in the rock.

At the base of the cliff, dark tunnels had been bored into the very foundations of the hill, and into them crawled gangs of men and women, fifty at a time, chained together at the waist, burdened down with drills and augers and pick-axes. Others pushed trucks full of rock along metal rails to a mill where, with earsplitting violence, great pile-drivers pulverised the rock.

'Are they convicts, or what?' breathed Hopeful.

'I don't think so,' Christian whispered back.

'But why else would they labour like that? Look at them! Breaking their backs! Sweating and straining like that! They'll be old before their time!'

'Ah, but the silver! There's always the silver to keep them going – the chance that today they'll get rich,' said Christian.

He looked sideways at her as he said it. She felt the look, and blushed.

From their hidden vantage point, they could also see Pluto Crat and Owen Ends, who had just reached the cliff-edge directly above the mine workings. Pluto Crat was pointing over the brink but, from where he stood, Owen Ends could not see the seams of silver Pluto Crat was describing. So he leaned further forward.

'Right down at the bottom, there,' said Crat's gestures. 'Criss-crossing the whole cliff face. It's there for anyone with eyes: great swathes of silver – enough to make a man like you rich for a thousand years!'

Owen Ends leaned out still further.

Whether Pluto Crat pushed him, or whether he simply overbalanced, the man in the otter-fur coat was suddenly falling – falling and screaming, screaming and falling. The noise of the mine working swallowed up his screams. No one broke off from their work. No one rushed to the spot where he landed. The mining of Lucre Hill went on uninterrupted, and Pluto Crat sauntered back down towards the highway, to look for more 'investors'.

Hopeful and Christian were back on the Way before he even got there, Hopeful running as if she had the Devil himself on her tail. Hands in her hair, mouth wide with horror, she sprinted blindly along, intent only on getting away.

By the time Christian caught her up, she had recovered herself enough to speak, enough to thank him over and over again. 'If you hadn't held me back,' she said repeatedly, 'I would've gone with Pluto Crat, and that would've been the end of me! Oh, thank you! Thank you!'

'Perhaps. Perhaps not,' said Christian. 'It's true what you said about money. Money could do a lot of good in the world. It's the *getting* of it . . . Getting it eats up time and energy and good intentions. Sometimes it even eats the heart out of a

person . . . And we have enough to see us through, don't we? You and I?'

See them through what? Neither Hopeful nor Christian knew what lay ahead, nor what resources they would need to carry them as far as the City of Gold. So instead they settled for a night's sleep in a meadow by a stream.

It was Christian's idea: his feet were blistered by the new, indestructible boots, and he thought the going would be softer on the flowery grass. The path across the meadow appeared to run in exactly the same direction as the Pilgrim's Way. It would simply be softer underfoot – and sweet-smelling, too, the daisies luminous in the failing light.

Rest comes rarely enough to pilgrims.

They were woken by the earth beneath them trembling, and by a voice which seemed to rip its way through the treetops like cannonfire.

'Earth, salt, fire and brim!
I smell the blood of a true pilgrim!
If any trespass hereabout,
He'll end his days in Castle Doubt!'

Nine

DOUBTING CASTLE

*In which Christian
and Hopeful are taken
prisoner and taste the
depths of Despair*

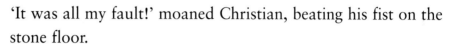

'It was all my fault!' moaned Christian, beating his fist on the stone floor.

Hopeful patted the darkness, trying to comfort her friend, but could not find him in the pitch black. Both had long since lost track of time; they only knew that for days on end they had been locked in the dungeon of Doubting Castle, without light or food or one drop to drink.

'All my fault!' wailed Christian again. 'I should never have suggested we walked on the grass! We should never have left the straight-and-narrow! Now look what I've brought you to!'

'Don't blame yourself,' said Hopeful. 'If it weren't for you, I would have got no further than Lucre Hill.'

Around them in the dark, cockroaches clicked and scurried. The stench was terrible, and it seemed as if the Giant had forgotten the very existence of prisoners in his dungeon.

At last, with a noise of rasping, oilless hinges, the door swung open. The light which fell like a blade across the soiled straw hurt their eyes.

'Still 'live, then?' said the Giant. 'Fort you mighta killed each other by now, quarrellin' 'bout who wuz to blame.'

'Of course not. We are friends,' said Hopeful. 'And our King will save us; we have every faith in that.'

'Your King?' The Giant threw back his head, knobbly as a cottage loaf, and laughed, showing three or four cheese-yellow teeth and a tongue like a flitch of bacon. 'None knows you's here! Strayed offa the King's 'ighway, din' you? Gived yoursel's inna my 'ands, din' you? Now you's in *my* keepin'! Heared tell, that King o' yourn died coupla thousan' year back. Ain't foolin' yousel's there's no Golden City at enda that road, is you? No such fing. Just a road goes round the world and back to wherevers you started.'

'We're poor pilgrims,' explained Hopeful. 'No one will pay a ransom for us. We're of no use to you as hostages. Why should you want to keep us here?'

The Giant shrugged his shoulders, an upheaval of grey flesh and hair, like an elephant sneezing. 'Don't mean to keep you 'ere,' he said. 'Mean for yous to *die*.'

Waiting to enjoy the impact of his words on the two prisoners, he was disappointed when the young female one replied boldly, 'We're not afraid of your kind, Sir Bully. We've been in worse places than this, and we've won through, with the help of our King!'

Giant Despair slammed the door shut again with such force that cockroaches showered down from the ceiling. Upstairs, his giant wife summoned him to bed by thumping the feather mattress beside her. She was whale-shaped and blubbery, her hair falling about her carcass like bladderwrack seaweed, her mouth round as a blowhole. 'How fare the prisoners, my bonny barnacle?'

'Not good, my little lumpen lovely. So far so fearless, I fear.'

'Then give 'em a clout or two with your club, sweeting, that's my advice. That will soon knock the courage outa them.'

The Giant followed his wife's advice and, next time he visited the dungeons, took with him his great club, made from a pollarded baobab tree. He laid about the prisoners mercilessly, clubbing them so hard that they fell on top of one another in a groaning heap. 'Despair and die, wormlings!' he said. 'My wife sends 'er salutations and says, "Why not kill yousel's? End will come quicker that way."'

This time he left a candle behind him and, ranged in niches around the cell wall, a variety of useful items – a rope, a knife and a bottle of poison.

'We have been in worse straits!' Hopeful shouted after him once more. 'We shall win through, with the help of our King!' But the Giant had gone. The silence of Doubting Castle bore down on them – a million tonnes of silent flint.

'When?' said Christian.

'When what?'

'When have we been in a worse situation than this? I only ask. I can't think of one, that's all.'

Hopeful did not reply, except to say, 'Bear up, my friend. Where there's life, there's hope!'

And where there's death, there's peace, thought Christian, though he did not speak the words out loud. Better to die now than give the Giant a week's, a fortnight's, a month's enjoyment tormenting them.

Next day the Giant came again, swinging his club like a woodman felling trees. 'What, not dead yet? You'll be sorry you din' take my wifey's kind advice. Not every warder shows his prisoners the way out, ha ha!'

'Suicide is the wickedest sin of all, as you perfectly well know,' retorted Hopeful defiantly. 'No true pilgrim would stoop to killing himself! Do your worst!'

But after the Giant and his club had finished with them, there was nothing either craved but the blessed release of Death.

Upstairs, the Giant's wife was starting to sulk. 'Shame on you, my hummocking lummock. Ain't those pilgrims despaired yet?'

'Not yet, lumpkin. I'm afeared we'll 'ave to eat 'em as they are, all stiff set in their ways and believing.'

'Booby baby!' growled the Giantess. 'You know the Enemy won't pay us the reward lessen they despair! Take 'em out the morrow and show 'em the bones of them men you've ripped asunder. That'll soften their haughtiness.'

'What a treasure you are to me,' said the Giant, tenderly stroking his wife's beard.

So next day, Hopeful and Christian were allowed to leave the terrible underground dungeon, weighted down with chains, and taken to the courtyard above, to see the whitening bones of those who had died in Doubting Castle. A whole xylophone of bones.

'Alla these pilgrims stayed till they grasped the Troof,' said the Giant. 'Troof is: they's nothing after Death but darkness and dust.'

His wife loomed at a window high above them, and waved a dirty handkerchief at the two pilgrims. 'Better off dead, my dearios!' she cried blithely. 'Better off dead!'

'Where there's life there's hope!' croaked Hopeful, though her throat was too dry for any sound to emerge.

But Christian said nothing. He had begun to wonder if it could be true, after all; if the Golden City could really be a fairy tale invented by the likes of Preacher and Owen Ends to justify their existence.

Hopeful knew what he was thinking. She also knew that, without Christian, she would be too young and too afraid to hold out against the Giant Despair.

When they returned to the dungeon, the chilly cold of the cell struck home very like despair, all but stifling the last spark within their pilgrim souls. Every sill and jut of stone was lined with pretty little bottles of coloured liquor: poison.

'It's not every gaoler give 'is prisoners the key to gettin' loose,' said the Giant, fond of repeating his macabre little joke. The door closed with a clang which knocked three of the bottles to the ground, where they broke, fumed and charred the straw.

'The key,' said Christian.

Hopeful sat up. There was something altered in the tone of Christian's voice.

'The key! That's it! Why didn't I think of it before? *I have the key*!' His eyes were bright in the candlelight. Hopeful resolved to smash all the bottles before her friend committed the unforgivable sin of taking his own life.

But Christian had lost all interest in the poison. He was fumbling inside his clothes now, looking for something. At last he pulled out a key. His injured fingers promptly dropped it – 'What a fool I am! What a clumsy fool!' – and they had to crawl about with the candle, searching the slimy flagstones, praying the flame would not blow out.

But there it was: the key which Preacher had given Christian along with the book and scroll, and which Christian had entirely forgotten. They held it up to the candlelight in order to read the words etched along the barrel of the key. These read:

'And lo, I am with you always,
even unto the end of the world.'

It slid into the keyhole as sweetly as oil, and the tumblers of the lock all turned at the touch of finger and thumb. The door swung open, and healing sunlight washed over them (though it had been raining moments before). There was no sign of the Giant or his grotesque wife, and the portcullis of Doubting Castle was firmly down. But Christian's key also opened the postern gate, and both pilgrims, though bruised and gasping, did not stop running till they reached the safety of the Pilgrim's Way.

'We must warn other pilgrims not to make the same mistake we did!' panted Hopeful, hands on knees, catching her breath.

So Christian piled together a cairn of stones, and on a big boulder alongside wrote:

Here be giants.
Nearby stands Doubting Castle.
Do NOT stray from the path.

Ten

THE DOOR IN THE HILLSIDE

In which the pilgrims reach the Delectable Mountains, like others before them

All at once they were among the foothills, and ahead of them rose snow-capped mountains. Purple and lilac rock slopes were interspersed with red and yellow gorse and alpine meadows of sweet grass oversprinkled with speedwell, forget-me-not and love-lies-bleeding. Sheep with fleeces of pristine whiteness grazed on every conceivable ledge and slope, with bells round their necks which rang out such pure notes that the breeze was ragged with music.

A group of shepherds were sitting round a hickory fire playing reed pipes and wood whistles, and the scene was so idyllic that at first Christian and Hopeful were unwilling to go forward; like dropping a pebble into a pool's reflection, they thought they might dispel the magic of this perfect place. But catching sight of them, the shepherds jumped up and beckoned them closer. Christian hesitated. 'Where exactly are we?' he asked tentatively.

'On the King's territory, sir. On the Delectable Mountains,' replied the oldest shepherd. 'The sheep you see are the King's sheep, and we, sir, are the King's shepherds.'

'Are we going the right way for the Golden City?' asked Hopeful.

'You are, if you don't turn aside from it.'

'How much further is it?' asked Christian.

'Too far – except for those who get there.'

'Is the way ahead safe?' asked Hopeful.

'Safe for those who come to no harm.'

Christian smiled wanly. He did not venture to ask about a bed for the night; he was not sure he would understand the answer. But when the pilgrims did not approach, the shepherds came over, smiling, taking them by the hands, leading them to the fireside.

There was fruit to eat, sheep's milk, cheese and fresh bread with raisins. Not until they met with such kindness did the pilgrims realise how wary they had become of strangers.

'Would you care to spend the night in our hut? Or will you sleep out under the stars?' asked the oldest shepherd. 'There are a pair of other pilgrims already staying with us. It's best for pilgrims to travel in company. Tomorrow you can all four set off together.'

As soon as Christian heard tell of other pilgrims, he was raring to meet them. Who could they be? Someone he had already met along the way? His parents, perhaps, having overtaken him while he lay in prison? Or someone else from his home town? Somebody escaped from Lucre Hill? Or broken free of Vanity Fair? He could not wait to find out.

But on the way down from the alp to the hut, they passed something so strange that it put everything else out of mind. There, in the side of the hill, was a little iron door, rattled and shaken by some force coming from within. A trickle of yellowish smoke crept out round the door frame, despite heavy bolts fastening it shut.

'What's in there?' asked Hopeful, intrigued.

'Oh, just the way back,' said the shepherds, who had grown accustomed to the presence of this extraordinary hatchway. 'Do you want to see?'

The pilgrims both held off at a cautious distance, unsure what lava or under-world demons might come rushing out when the door was opened. But the shepherds pulled the cuffs of their sleeves down to protect their hands, and casually shot the hot bolts. No horned demons or impish ghouls streamed out, no bubbling tar. There was just a chute of blackness on the other side, a tunnel falling away into Nothingness, a fast route to Nowhere. 'Many's the pilgrim will come within sight of the Golden City only to end his journey here,' said the shepherd, letting the iron hatch-way fall back into place with a clang.

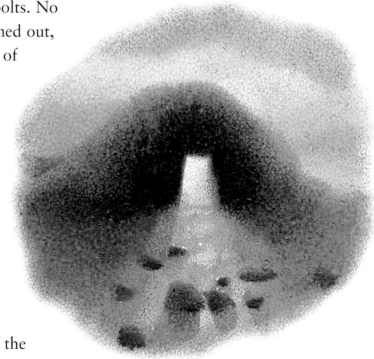

'Are we?' said Hopeful.

'Destined for All or Nothing? Bless me, child! Who am I to know a thing like that?'

'No, I meant are we within sight of the Golden City?'

'Oh yes, miss! With a spyglass, miss. Why? Would you care to look?'

Would they care to look? These shepherds had lived so long among the delights of the Delectable Mountains that they had forgotten what such a sight could mean to a weary pilgrim.

The shepherds possessed a spyglass; they even led Christian and Hopeful to the top of a hill and told them which way to look.

'You look, Christian,' said Hopeful. 'My eyes are so poor. You look!'

But the sight of that door in the hillside, the *thought* of that door in the hillside, the *fact* of that door in the hillside, had struck such fear into Christian that his hands shook as he held the telescope up to his eye.

'What can you see?' said Hopeful eagerly. 'Can you see it? Can you? What is it like? Describe it!'

Christian lowered the spyglass, blinked away tears of frustration and tried again. But his shaking hands blurred the image into a smudge of circular light.

'Just a brightness, my dear. Just a brightness.'

The shepherds' lodge nestled under a grass-turfed roof, beside a bubbling spring. There were fleeces on the beds, and broth cooking over the turf fire. Two pilgrims looked up when Christian and Hopeful entered; Christian knew them instantly. Though there were other people he would rather have met up with, he was relieved to see they had not perished as he feared. 'You won't know Mr Smug and Miss Stake,' he said, introducing them to Hopeful. 'I met them at the Hill. They went round the base of the Hill; I went over the top. That's how we lost touch. I was worried for you, Miss Stake. The signpost said that primrose path of yours led to DANGER. I was afraid you might come to harm.'

'Fooh! The signpost to *my* path said DESTRUCTION,' snorted Smug, 'but you see I'm still here! I'm not as gullible as some. *Some* people like to make hard work out of everything. I told you: the great thing is to be on the Way: it doesn't matter how you get there.'

'So you still don't have scrolls to present at the Golden City,' said Christian, and he could see Hopeful's eyes widen in dismay at hearing this.

'Don't you worry about us. We'll get in,' said Miss Stake. 'I'm not a bad woman, me . . . You got rid of your burden, I see. I 'spect you left off carrying that great heavy book of yours, too. It's like Smug said: only fools do things the hard way. Best to travel light.'

Hopeful's eyes widened still further, but seeing that Christian was not in a mood to argue, she too kept silent.

After weeks of captivity in Doubting Castle, the shepherds' hut was a haven of comfort (though they slept with the door ajar, as prisoners do who are trying to forget confinement).

Next morning, Hopeful and Christian rose early. Christian wanted to get on the road before the other two woke because (as he admitted in a guilty whisper) he found it hard to be civil to either of them. Hopeful was rather relieved to hear this: she had thought there must be something uncharitable about her that she liked Smug and Stake so little.

The shepherds, however, were already up and about, and warned Christian against setting off alone. 'The country between here and the River is rife with bandits. You would do much better travelling together. Didn't you hear tell what Little Faith went through?'

'No, what happened to him?'

'Just after he left here, he was set upon by a gang of robbers. They beat him up and stole all his money – cloak clasp, belt buckle, everything. They only stopped short of killing him because they heard someone coming and thought it might be the King's Champion. Luckily, Little Faith had sewn his scroll into the lining of his jacket, so the robbers didn't get that. And they threw his guidebook

aside as being too heavy. But of course the theft left him with no means of buying food – and it's a district where nobody gives you anything except for hard cash.'

'The fool could always have sold his book or scroll or something,' said Smug, who had woken up in time to hear this story.

'In those parts there's no market for such things,' said the shepherd. 'No, he just had to go hungry. And his nerves were shot to pieces. He lived in permanent terror of being attacked again; dwelt on his misfortune more and more, until he convinced himself he was just not *meant* to reach the Golden City. Those robbers were almost the undoing of him.'

'The man was a fool to travel alone,' said Smug complacently. 'I don't intend to budge from here unless I know I'm safe from any fool of a footpad.' To Smug, the world was full of fools. The shepherds, the Enemy, the bandits, his fellow travellers, they were all fools.

'Who is this "King's Champion"?' asked Hopeful suddenly. 'You mentioned the "King's Champion". Said the bandits were scared of him.'

'Oh yes. They're scared right enough!' said the shepherd and, for the first time, even he seemed in awe. 'There *are* travellers who could walk from here to the Golden City without so much as a straw hat to keep off the bandits. First sign of trouble and they'd whistle up the King's Champion. One whistle and they'd know he would come hurtling down the lanes on his white mare – lance up, visor down – and scatter the villains like so many horseflies. Little Faith could have whistled. Oh yes. But he didn't have the confidence. He wasn't certain in his own mind, you know, whether the Champion would sink his lance in the bandits or in him? You have to have nerves of steel to whistle up the King's Champion – though he's there, right enough, waiting, always on patrol.'

As the four pilgrims filed out of the shepherds' hut and set off along the last few miles of the Pilgrim's Way, Christian observed, 'My friend Faithful now, *he* would have whistled. I know him. He would have whistled without thinking twice.'

'And you?' said Hopeful.

'Not me. I'm too much like Little Faith. I'd never be sure whether the King's Champion would come to my rescue or to teach me a lesson.' And his eyes lingered on the smoking black door in the hillside, which they were just then passing.

Overhearing him, Smug called Christian a fool and a villain. 'You should have led a better life, then. Me, I haven't put a foot wrong since I was a child. I've obeyed all the rules, never broken a law, always done my duty. We're not talking Luck here. I know my rights and privileges. I'm *entitled* to protection from the King's Champion, whoever he is. If you're going to succeed in this life, it's just a matter of following the right and proper procedures, and keeping one's nose clean. Of course that takes a certain degree of *intelligence*,' he added, with heavy sarcasm, looking Hopeful up and down as if she were something he had found on the sole of his boot.

'I'm not sure if I'd whistle or not,' said Hopeful to Christian, unabashed. 'But I hope we catch a glimpse of this "King's Champion" along the way.'

'Oh well, then,' Smug interrupted sardonically, 'perhaps I should oblige the lady.' He puckered up his lips.

But he never blew.

Hopeful had barely spoken, when the drumming of hooves set little birds pluming out of the trees, and squirrels leaping for upper branches. The King's Champion did not come alone, but with outriders in robes of white, with cloaks, or something similar, furled tightly down their backs. They carried a length of chain between them.

The pilgrims scattered. Only Smug was left standing in the middle of the road. The white mare brushed against him and passed by. A grin of reassurance spread over Smug's face: the King's Champion was simply riding by. Then the chain caught him beneath the armpits, and he was lifted clear off the ground.

It all happened so fast that, by the time the others took stock, Smug was bound round in a dozen turns of chain and hoisted across the rump of the Champion's horse. His face emerged from under the chequered saddlecloth for a moment, astonished, protesting. His lips shaped themselves over and over again into his favourite word: *Fool!*

'Let me go, you fools! You're making a terrible mistake!' But the riders were under strict orders to convey Smug to the door in the hillside. His travelling companions saw the arch of dark, as the bolted door was thrown open and Smug was posted, feet-first and screaming, down the chute to Nothingness.

'So his road did lead to Destruction, after all,' said Hopeful, thinking aloud.

The King's Champion did not turn back to explain himself. His outriders spurred their horses to a gallop, then a new, oppressive silence fell over the Pilgrim's Way.

'I'm so sorry,' Christian said to Miss Stake, as soon as he could manage to speak at all. 'I'm so very . . .'

Miss Stake shrugged. She puffed out her cheeks and let the air escape in an expression of irritable indifference. 'No great loss,' she said, tossing her hair back off her face. 'He was a fool anyway.'

Eleven

AMBUSH

*In which Christian
and Hopeful are
ambushed, and meet
a lifelong traveller*

Along the way, they came to a fork in the road. This time there was no straight way ahead, no signpost to tell them which way they should turn.

'Goodness sakes alive! And haven't you done well now?' said a kindly, broguish voice. A gentleman sat beneath a tree peeling an apple. 'The Golden City is going to be mighty pleased to have three pilgrims of your calibre!'

Miss Stake took an instant dislike to the Irishman. 'He wants something,' she warned. 'He's a beggar. Beggars are always polite. I don't give to beggars; it encourages them.'

Christian and Hopeful (who gave often and often to beggars) flinched from her loud and uncharitable rudeness, but the gentleman did not seem put out. 'Your road lies that way,' he said. 'But sure you don't need me to tell you that. Seasoned pilgrims like you, you begin to *sense* the right and proper way, isn't that the truth of it?'

Miss Stake persisted in her belief he was a beggar. 'He wants something for telling us the way. You mark my words! He probably sits here all day every day, scrounging off pilgrims; knows we're a soft touch.' And so, out of a mixture of mistrust and sheer contrariness, she stamped away down the left-hand road. Hopeful and Christian called after her, 'I think we'll go the other way. Take care! Safe journey! See you in the City!'

Miss Stake herrumphed and quickened her step, her only response a muttered, 'Good riddance.'

'I'm sorry about that,' said Hopeful.

'Don't worry about it,' said the gentleman with the apple. 'She went the wrong way, anyway – as you sensible people perfectly well know.' He jumped to his feet with great agility. 'Come with me, won't you? My house is an easy step along the road. Might I maybe dare to offer you a refreshing drink in exchange for hearing some of the wisdom you have gained along the way? Me, I'm a man thirsty for wisdom, and I can see you two have plenty; it's written on your faces.'

Christian strode out along the right-hand road, singing and turning his face to the sun, considering what he could say of help and instruction to their hospitable guide. The Irishman (he could hear) was complimenting Hopeful on how clean she had kept her dress. '. . . it's surely plain you didn't fall into the Great Bog . . .' he heard, and Hopeful was laughing, gratified.

Suddenly, Christian's shin met with something invisible in the roadway: a trip-wire stretched between two trees. It relented with a twang, and the leaves covering the path leapt up all around, in a rustling like applause.

'Look out!' he shouted. But Hopeful was too close behind him and, when the net concealed by the leaves rose up to engulf him, she too was snared. They were pitched against each other and lifted clear off the ground, their fingers and faces scored by the harsh mesh of the net. Like a brace of pheasant they hung, bagged up and helpless, while the gentleman with the apple punched and slapped at them, set them swinging like a pendulum, lashed at them with a broken tree branch, poked them with his paring knife.

'You arrogant, self-satisfied little prigs,' he mouthed, pushing his handsome face up close. 'Ready to believe anything *good* about yourselves, aren't you? Always ready to think well of yourselves! Well, O'Flattery's got you in his net now, and O'Flattery is seeking to teach you a lesson in humility!'

Hopeful tried to whistle, but her mouth was soft with crying; she could not pucker it into a round enough sound. 'Whistle, Christian! Whistle! Summon the King's Champion!'

But Christian only writhed and groaned and screwed his face into an even worse grimace than the netting carved on it. 'I deserve it. I deserve it. The Champion wouldn't come for me! Why would he come? He'd come for you,

but why would anyone come to the aid of a vain, jumped-up little coxcomb like me?'

They shut their eyes. They submitted to the spite and vindictiveness of their ambusher, until he wearied of his game and left them, hanging in their black chrysalis of net, swinging through sickening arcs of pain, several miles along the wrong forest path.

'Wrong path? Wrong path! When will you people realise: there's no such thing as a *right* path,' brayed the shabby, ragged man who came along at last and cut them down. He came strolling through the trees and cut them loose with a pocket knife, but all that time he wore a look of amused disgust, shaking his head at the sound of the same old story. He had heard it all so many times before.

'It doesn't exist, you know,' he said, as they slithered head-first out of the net. 'What doesn't?' Hopeful hugged her knees, nursing her injuries.

'The City of Gold. It doesn't exist. All my life I've travelled up and down these lanes. Once, I was like you – searching for it all the time, expecting to find it over the next hill and the next. But it never was. Just the same old mixture of good and evil, good folk and villains. Fifty years I've been travelling about. Believe me: if it was there, I'd've found it by now. It's a fiction. A fairy tale. It's wishful thinking.

There's nothing at the end of the road but the start of the road back. Save yourself the trip, that's my advice. Take it from me who knows.'

'Who? Who are you, then? What's your name?' demanded Hopeful angrily. 'Did the Enemy send you to discourage people with your lies?'

Atheist (for that was his name) only laughed. 'The Enemy? He's a fairy tale, too. No Heaven and no Hell. No King and no Enemy. And still you keep coming, you people. Day after day, year after year; the credulous in pursuit of the incredible. Why can't you just accept the proof? I've looked for a lifetime, and it just isn't there!'

The sight of them sitting on the ground, ready to argue, but with no ready argument to give, made him laugh all the more – laugh and laugh. But there was a bitter metallic edge to his laughter which put them in mind of hyenas, or gibbons hooting.

'You can't prove a negative!' Hopeful called after him, as Atheist walked off, still shaking with mirthless laughter. 'No one can prove a thing *doesn't* exist! It's a scientific impossibility!'

Atheist turned for a moment and looked back, his laugh dislodged like a pair of spectacles. He spread his big hands to either side of his body, inviting them to look his shabbiness up and down. '*I am* the proof, you poor deluded noodles. I *am* the proof!'

Twelve

THE
VALLEY OF THE SHADOW

In which the pilgrims cross enchanted ground and enter the most feared place of all

They thought at first that it was heat haze rising off the poppy fields – or hordes of tiny flies. But it was sleep – a stupefaction of sleepiness, an intoxication of drowsiness, an enchantment.

'Let's just lie down here and rest,' said Hopeful. 'I can't go another step.'

'No. No. We mustn't sleep. I made that mistake once before, and it lost me my scroll. Keep awake! We must keep awake! Step out lively, now. There's something sinister about this place. I smell magic.'

But Hopeful was swaying, dizzy with the effects of the poppies, and Christian had to put one arm around her, or she would have swooned, then and there, among the flowers. Clouds of pollen burst upwards in their faces as her skirts swept the papery petals loose from their stems. He himself longed to fall headlong among the fallen petals, and surrender to sleep.

'Sing, Hopeful! Come on now, sing! That'll keep us awake!'

So they sang:

'He who would valiant be 'gainst all disaster,
let him in constancy follow the Master!
There's no discouragement
shall make him once relent
his first avowed intent
to be a pilgrim!'

Anyone watching would have mistaken them for revellers reeling home from an inn.

'Who so beset him round with dismal stories
do but themselves confound; his strength the more is!
No foes shall stay his might,
Though he with giants fight:
he will make good the right
to be a pilgrim!'

'Do you know any riddles?' whispered Hopeful. 'Ask me a riddle. Perhaps a riddle will keep me awake.'

'All right. What do you call a ram caught by its horns in a thicket?'

'I don't know; what do you call a ram caught by its horns?'

'A sheepwreck. What do you call a pilgrim in the wilderness?'

'I don't—'

'Lost.'

But Hopeful's head lolled forward on to her chest, and her breathing became heavy.

'Hopeful, wake up! What do you call a pilgrim who falls asleep?'

'I—'

'Anything, SO LONG AS YOU CALL IT LOUD ENOUGH!' Christian bellowed in her ear. She recoiled from the noise, covering her ear and frowning at him.

'Let's have a quiz!' said Christian, himself swerving with dizziness, as the poppies blew round his knees. 'How do you recognise a Christian?'

'Is this a riddle?' asked Hopeful.

'No. Pay attention. It's a quiz. How do you know a Christian?'

Hopeful screwed up her face in concentration. '"*By his works ye shall know him*",' she said, quoting from the guidebook. 'My turn. How do you recognise a friend?'

It was Christian now who frowned with perplexity. He opened his guidebook, but did not know where to begin looking.

'I'll tell you,' offered Hopeful. 'He's the one who keeps you awake on enchanted ground.' She gave a wry smile, and together they steered a wavering course for the edge of the field. 'I hope no one sees us,' said Hopeful ruefully. 'They'll think we've been drinking strong liquor, and I've never held with that.'

Suddenly, Christian tripped over something hidden under the dense tarpaulin of flowers. It was Miss Stake sleeping, curled up, as soundly as a cat in a basket.

Christian took her head, and Hopeful her legs, and after that it was the sheer physical effort of carrying the sleeping pilgrim which kept them awake as far as the edge of the poppy field.

'She'll be safe now,' said Christian. 'Shall we set her down here, and go? I suspect she prefers to travel alone.'

'She doesn't like us, you mean,' said Hopeful bluntly. 'But are you sure she'll be all right?'

They looked around them. Bandit country was past. Enchantment had lost its power. The countryside blossomed in sunlit splendour. Any seams of silver here were trout streams; the only castle keeps were towering chestnut trees; its bandits were brightly coloured jays and dapper magpies; its net-snares were cobwebs hung with dew. Loud birdsong was accompanied by the bowing of crickets. Yes, Miss Stake would be safe here. They left her sleeping on the plush grass, and went on their way, singing just for the pleasure of it:

'. . . *Then fancies flee away!*
I'll fear not what men say,
I'll labour night and day
to be a pilgrim!'

Christian and Hopeful passed the sweetest days of their pilgrimage walking through the Land of Beulah, their happiness increasing daily until their hearts ached with it – ached, too, with wistfulness at the fleeting nature of life and of summer days. More and more often, Christian laid his hand to his chest and stopped walking, to recover his breath, oppressed by happiness.

'Are you well, Christian?' Hopeful would ask, and he would nod. Nor was he so distracted by his own feelings that he did not see the changes in Hopeful – the greying of her hair, the deepening of lines in her face. They did not hurry onwards out of the Land of Beulah. They seemed to have all the time in the world to dawdle on their way.

And then one day they looked around, and everything had changed. Bare granite hills swelled like tumours out of the ground, enclosing them in a fearful glen. Down this vale funnelled icy, whistling winds which bled the colour out of the landscape without ever dispersing the cloud overhead. For where there should have been sky, whole generations of bleak black clouds had piled up, excluding all possibility of sun. The only light which ever shone in the Valley of the Shadow was the fitful flash of lightning and the flare of raging fires. Though there was no vegetation to burn, these fires crawled inexorably about the granite slopes, adding

their own hollow roar to the noise of the wind.

But the worst noise in the Valley of the Shadow was of crying.

What at first sight had seemed to Christian and Hopeful an empty, inert void, was in fact as swarming with people as an anthill is aswarm with ants. Some were simply old; others were sick – delirious with fever or doubled up with pain; some diseased, some insane. Soldiers and civilians, casualties of war, lay about calling for someone to tend their wounds. The drowning called from beneath frozen sheets of water. The starving held out empty bowls, pleading with empty eyes.

There were even children.

Hopeful's first thought was to go to them – to help. But Christian restrained her in the nick of time. She had not seen what he had – that to either side of the Pilgrim's Way was a deep, deep trench. There was no leaving the path; indeed, it was so narrow that they could not so much as turn round to go back.

All the while, the dying called out to them, imploring them less often for help than for an explanation. '*Why?*' they kept repeating. '*Why?*' and '*Why me?*'

'Why must it be like this?'

'What is the King thinking of?'

'Why does he allow it?'

'What did I do to deserve this?'

'Doesn't the King care?'

'Isn't he supposed to come when we call?'

'They told us he was loving and kind!'

'*Why?*'

Christian summoned up all his courage. But these were not lions on either side of his path; it was not simply a matter of shutting his eyes and ears and rushing past. Courage was no good to him here.

Hopeful summoned up all her energy and determination. But there was no foe to fight here, no hard labour to be endured, no temptation to be withstood. Determination was no good to her here.

Christian fumbled through his guidebook, but there was nothing in it to help him answer that incessant cry of *Why? Why? Why?* Wisdom was no good to him here.

Hopeful mustered all her reserves of charity and pity, but the trenches stopped her reaching anyone to help them. Besides, pity was futile. Pity was one drop of water thrown at a raging bonfire. It was of no use in the world to these poor dying souls. No. Pity and good works were no good to anyone here.

Nothing remained but to pray. Christian and Hopeful prayed – not *for* anything, but just prayed. They did it instinctively, blindly, like children going through the motions, repeating words they had recited all their lives. In this terrible place, there was nothing left to do but pray:

'*Yea, though I walk through the Valley of the Shadow of Death, I will fear no evil; for thou art with me; thy rod and thy staff they comfort me. Surely goodness and mercy shall follow me all the days of my life; and I will dwell in the house of the Lord for ever.*'

And praying brought them through. The glen opened up on to rich, cultivated countryside: a colourful patchwork of fields seemingly stitched together with twining vines. A fine mist lay over everything, such as hangs over the world before full sunrise burns it away. Christian and Hopeful pulled clusters of grapes from the vines to cram against their mouths. The shadowy figures moving among the vines (barely visible in the mist because they were dressed in white) did not object, but smiled encouragingly and pointed further on, as if there were even better things in store . . .

Christian shook his head, but the noise in his ears, which he had thought was his own excited pulse, only grew louder. He realised that he was listening to the sound of a rushing river.

Suddenly Hopeful was tugging on his sleeve, pointing, gasping. 'There it is, Christian! There it is! The City! We've done it! We've arrived!'

What he had mistaken for morning light was not coming from the sun, but from the shining walls of the City of Gold. It stood almost directly in front of them – not above three miles away. Its outline was clearly visible!

Christian began to run. Hopeful ran, too, still clutching her friend's sleeve. They would be there in an hour or so! Nothing could keep them from reaching it now!

The noise of rushing water grew louder. Spray began to wet their faces with tiny droplets of cold – like a clammy sweat. Their run came to an abrupt halt as the Pilgrim's Way reached its end. This straight and narrow pathway, trodden white by the traffic of a million feet, brought them at last to a river bank.

And there is no bridge across the Final River.

Thirteen

ONE MORE RIVER

*In which Christian
and Hopeful sink
or swim*

'Cross over,' said a voice behind them. 'The water is cold, but the prize is worth it.' It was one of the white-clothed farmers; he seemed surprised they should hesitate, even for a moment.

'Is the water very deep?' asked Christian.

'Here and there.'

'Can we ford it on foot?' said Hopeful.

'It's deeper in some places than others,' the farmer repeated. 'It depends what faith you have in surviving. One way or another, you have to try and cross. Everyone does.'

They tried to see, from the bank, where it would be best to cross, but the water boiled downstream, muddy, tormented by currents into whirlpools and eddies, breaking foam, and rafts of swirling flotsam. Hopeful sat down and dangled her feet in the rushing water, then, holding one hand over nose and mouth, bravely slipped off the bank into the River.

The water came up to her neck. Her grizzled hair, coming unfastened, spread round her on the water as she grinned encouragingly up at Christian. So he, too, slid into the water.

The cold robbed him of breath and all power to speak. He thought his heart would burst inside him. And he found no reassuring bed of pebbles under his feet – only coiling manacles of weed which imprisoned his legs and overbalanced him. The water closed over his head, and it was untold aeons before he struggled to the

surface and pushed his face into the sunny air. 'I'm drowning! Save me!' he gasped.

'Don't panic, Christian,' said Hopeful, fighting the current to reach him. 'Come towards me. There's solid ground where I am! You can walk across!'

'No! No! I'll drown! I'll drown! I know it!' and he clung to the overhanging bank, though it broke off in clods and tussocks, muddying his face. He could not climb out again.

Glancing upstream, his eyeballs bulged with apoplectic grief. *'It wasn't the only way!'* he gasped, pointing so wildly that he lost his footing again. *'It wasn't the only way. We were deceived again!'*

There, hardly a stone's-throw upstream, Miss Stake was just climbing into a ferry boat. How daintily she did it, helped aboard by the outstretched hand of a ferryman in a long cloak and enveloping hood. Christian waded towards the boat, clinging to tree roots in the bank, trying to hail the ferryman, trying to make Miss Stake see him. But his cries were washed away by the roar of the rushing River, and the current was too strong to push against. He only got close enough to hear the imperious tones of Miss Stake:

'. . . I'm not a bad woman, me . . .' and to read the name of the ferry boat painted across its transom.

Vain Hope, it said.

Miss Stake seated herself in the stern, and the ferryman pulled away from the bank, cutting strongly cross-stream. He quickly reached the other side, shipping his oars and alighting at a wooden jetty. 'Now. If I might see your scroll?' he asked Miss Stake.

'Unfortunately, I lost it,' she replied. 'That's to say, I was not issued with . . . I mean to say – an administrative error, actually. Anyway, I'm not a bad woman. I think I can honestly say, hand on heart, that I've always been a good woman, always done my duty, always played by the rules. I've done nothing to actually *require* forgiveness, so you see, I won't be needing any scroll.'

Without another word, the ferryman let go the painter of the little boat, and pushed it off from the jetty with his foot.

'What are you doing? Just a moment!' The boat rocked wildly, as Miss Stake tried to scramble ashore. But she was too late, and had (for fear of upsetting the boat) to cower back in the stern, as *Vain Hope* was carried back into midstream.

Faster and faster it floated, heeling and plunging among the knotty currents, until it turned side-on to a swollen wave and capsized in a welter of spray. Just once, Miss Stake's head and hand broke surface; her mouth was open:

'. . . *didn't need forgiving!*'

Then she sank from sight, and the River swept her away, as far and further than the Valley, the Mine, the Castle, the Hill or even the City of Destruction.

Christian was so spellbound with horror that he lost his grip on the bank and plunged out of his depth. Water swilled in at his mouth and nose and eyes. He was floundering, failing, drowning.

'Reach out to me! Give me your hand!' called Hopeful. 'I'm on solid ground!'

'No! No! I'd only drag you under. You cross over. Leave me. I'm done for.' He was rolling now in the water, a carcass, sodden, heavy.

'Look yonder, Christian! Look at the City! That's where we're going! Soon we'll be there! Just keep your eyes on the City! Make for the City! Don't think about anything else!'

He could see it, too, his unreachable goal. It had golden walls – not made of mere precious metal, but of some diaphanous gold – the substance of sunlight forged into buttress and curtain-wall, into keep and donjon and belltower. Countless people were streaming up the hill from the River towards an adamantine portcullis, where banners of white and red cloth idly curled and unfurled above the gatehouse. On one golden dome rested the Moon, on another the Sun, while stars rode like embers on the updraught of light.

But not for Christian. He had doubted in Doubting Castle. He had dwelt on the words of Atheist. He had not been able to answer the questions of the dying: *why?*

He rolled face-down, face-up, hands adrift in the churning turmoil of the River. Hopeful waded over to him, put her arms around his head, and supported it, so that his face was at least above the surface, though water washed over his features with every wave.

'You always had more faith than I did, Hopeful!' gasped Christian. 'Only you are meant to reach the City! I all but led you astray. This is as far as I go.'

But Hopeful would not give up. Even when Christian almost lost consciousness and was talking wild nonsense about demons and fire, she drew him through the water, whispering to him soothingly of glory and everlasting peace. 'This is only Death, Christian. That's all. It comes to each of us. But it isn't the end for us! We're pilgrims, we have further to go. We have to get to the City. We are expected! We have the best to come!'

All of a sudden, hands were grasping them, helping them, steadying them, lifting them ashore. Teams of angels, their breeches rolled up past the knee, sleeves pushed back, stood in the shallows to lend a pair of strong arms where they were needed and to welcome the pilgrims ashore; to wrap them each in a robe of soft white wool (for they were naked) and towel their hair into electric clouds of crackling gold.

No, Hopeful's hair was no longer grey, her face no longer lined. It was as though the River had washed away all signs of sorrow and hardship and age. Christian knew for himself that the River washed away all pain, too.

They all but ran the last few yards.

The River had taken all their clothing – stripped it off their backs, along with the dregs of Christian's battered armour. It had even ripped their guidebooks out of their grasp. But somehow, through it all, their fists had stayed closed around their scrolls. By what miracle was that? By what miracle was the ink not smeared and smudged when the angel-guard at the City Gate unrolled these certificates of safe passage?

'Enter, pilgrims,' said the guard, beaming. 'Enter into your rightful home – and welcome!'

There was no triumphant roll of drums, no trumpet blast or herald announcing Christian and Hopeful. It was like market day, with motley crowds converging all the while on the city in huge numbers. But there was an air of celebration and exultation, of festival and fun. People began to dance in the streets out of sheer joy, and Christian and Hopeful joined in. There was a smell of rose petals and of cooking food; laughter spilled out of every window they passed. They caught sight of Little Faith sitting on the steps of a fountain, eating strawberries, and old friends hailed each other continuously from opposite sides of the square.

Naturally, Faithful had come to meet them.

'What a time you've taken getting here!' he said, as they walked, arm-in-arm, up a tree-lined avenue. 'Your mother and father arrived weeks ago, Christian!'

There was no hurry to reach the palace, no scramble to witness sights beyond imagining. All Eternity remained. Time encircled them, in a seamless circle of perfection, without beginning or end.

I cannot describe what Christian saw when he came face to face with the King, nor what Hopeful felt when all her hopes were fulfilled. I woke too soon.